THE ICARUS THREAT

BY THE SAME AUTHOR:

A BORDERLINE CASE
DOUBLE EXPOSURE

THE ICARUS THREAT

by

HUGH McLEAVE

LONDON
VICTOR GOLLANCZ LTD
1984

© Hugh McLeave 1984

British Library Cataloguing in Publication Data
McLeave, Hugh
　The Icarus threat.
　I. Title
　823'.914[F]　　　PR6063.A249

ISBN 0-575-03400-9

Photoset in Great Britain by
Rowland Phototypesetting Limited, Bury St Edmunds, Suffolk
and printed by St Edmundsbury Press
Bury St Edmunds, Suffolk

*For Pierre and
Claire-Lise Gandar*

I

BRODIE HAD LIVED long enough in this strange valley to consider age and time relative matters; yet, he could not help marvelling as he watched the spare, lithe figure of Bahadur Ali quick-striding up the sheer path towards the terrace where he sat working. Although well over ninety, the wazir of Hunza climbed like someone forty years younger and was easily outstripping the stranger who accompanied him. As they emerged from the mud-brick houses, which had apricots drying on their roofs like golden sovereigns, Brodie noticed that the old governor was wearing an immaculate shirt over his Punjabi-trousers and was also sporting his black waistcoat with its gold and silver filigree. That meant today was Friday and Bahadur Ali would be leading prayers at the mosque later in the morning and would officiate at the polo match that afternoon. Hearing the two men's salaams, Shane came out of the clinic where she had just finished treating a couple of Hunza children for minor ailments. Bahadur Ali and the stranger made courtly bows to her, then shook Brodie's hand.

"This man is Ikhbal Khan, who is headman from Sherkut village," Bahadur Ali said in English. "He is coming to tell of strange sickness in Runghar village, near our northern border."

"Has he, himself, seen the sickness, or anybody with it?" Shane asked.

When the wazir translated, Ikhbal Khan shook his head, saying a shepherd had brought the news. According to this second-hand account, every one of the Runghar villagers had fallen ill and the place looked dead; he had thought well to inform the sahib and mem-sahib in Hunza since they had saved his own son from death.

Brodie disappeared indoors to return with ordnance maps of the Hunza region. These he spread on the big stone table. Both the small oases of Sherkut and Runghar lay a few miles apart on the

Chapursan River which ran almost parallel with the Afghanistan border a little way north. At that point, Afghanistan narrowed to a thin corridor wedged between Pakistan, Soviet Russia and China's forbidden province of Sinkiang. Brodie moved a forefinger along these borders then lifted his head to gaze quizzically at Shane and the wazir.

"If you are thinking it is to do with the fighting on the other side and if you are wishing, I am informing Pakistan military doctors at Gilgit," the wazir murmured, interpreting Brodie's glance.

"What do you say, Shane?"

"They'll take another two days and it may be too late already," she replied. "We must go."

"Then I am telling to get three of our best ponies ready," Bahadur Ali said, and with another bow to Shane, he tripped downhill towards the new Hunza capital, Karimabad, to arrange their transport. Brodie and Shane started to pack some of their small supply of medicine—antibiotics and sulpha drugs they picked up, free, in Gilgit from the army medical officers, their painkillers, chloroquine antimalarials and several drugs for treating dysentery. Quizzing the headman in his elementary Urdu yielded no more clues about the illness, except that it had hit the village like an avalanche. Shigo, their constant companion, who had attached himself to them as their Hunza seneschal, got together rations for two weeks and ran downhill to bring back the three ponies to the disused palace which the wazir had allotted them as a home and clinic.

Within an hour they were ready to move. With their supplies, Shigo had packed tents, poshteens (thick sheepskin clothing), woollen jumpers and felt trousers stinking of linseed oil. For, though it was high summer, the mountains hemming them in lay encased in glaciers and snow, and temperatures could plummet from a broiling fifty degrees above zero in the afternoon to thirty below in the short nights. And those deep and dark gorges leading into and out of Hunza foamed with glacier water at this season.

Having gone over the check-list, Brodie sat down on the terrace to drink the coffee Shane had made them. He never wearied of the view over this wonderful valley; from their rocky falaise, the terraced fields tumbled downwards through Baltit and through Karimabad to the silver ribbon of the Hunza River. From there, a wall of mountains ended in eternal snow and beyond and above towered the immense pyramid of Rakaposhi mountain, barring the southern horizon. Now, sunlight was shimmering on its frozen waterfalls and streaming through the clouds ruffing round its summit. Brodie's eyes shifted to the emerald oasis of Hunza where farmers were toiling among apricot and peach orchards or harvesting early barley and wheat. It looked like a vast garden with its willows and poplars and chinars and its hundreds of varieties of wild flowers, roses, irises, oleander and hibiscus.

Just over two years ago, on emerging from the southern gorges, his first sight of this lost valley had halted him and he did not wonder that it had served as the model for Shangri-la, the never-never country where people lived well beyond the normal life-span and rarely fell ill. How did the Shangri-la legend run? Those who had decided to remain in the valley should never leave it. If they did, they would wither and die. Symbolic, like all legends, perhaps. Yet, time and the pace of life did seem to flow more slowly here, in this high and dry cordillera. At the rare visitors who wanted to measure his age in days or years or decades, Bahadur Ali merely laughed, treating time as a human artifice. His Hunza people had no more than their needs, they laboured long hours and lived on a staple diet of stone-ground flour, vegetables, their apricots and other fruits and little meat; but they were happy and they knew nothing of civilization and its stress diseases.

Brodie looked at Shane. Without make-up and wearing a rough shirt and jeans, she looked the antithesis of the medical research worker he had met when he arrived here. Her face had lost its taut lines, her skin glowed, her dark hair shone and she looked like a woman in her mid-twenties rather than ten years older. She caught his glance.

"What do you think it is, Paul?"

He shrugged. "Probably the usual—amoebic dysentery."

"In that case, we'll be a week at the most."

Was she echoing his thoughts, grudging the hours spent outside the valley? Or did she merely resent this interruption of their research project to discover why the twenty-five thousand Hunzas remained so healthy?

Brodie hoisted her on to the one unloaded pony and led them down the steep track into the valley. Twice they had to cross the Hunza River before plunging into the dark canyons that led west then due north. There, they had to feel their way along a narrow ledge above the river, eyes fixed on the sheer gorge in case an avalanche threatened them. With the river booming and echoing, no-one could speak as they plodded on hour after hour. Just after noon, where the gorge broke into a clearing, they stopped and Shigo made their lunch of boiled eggs and thick chupattis. Brodie gave a hand and the Hunza grinned at him. "You are remembering, Paul-sahib?" he said.

Yes, he remembered. His SIS bosses in London had sent him into this little hole where Dr Shane Kingslake had set up a World Health Organization unit to find the answer to a lethal virus that had decimated a village. Under his cover as a lab technician with the WHO, Brodie had to investigate mysterious earth tremors from suspected underground nuclear testing on the Chinese side. However, he soon realized that the virus posed the real threat—if the Chinese succeeded in taming and using it as a biological weapon. He had persuaded Shane to co-operate with him and prevent this. Shigo had lived the whole of that adventure with them. Captured from this rest-house and led into Sinkiang they discovered that Chinese nuclear explosions had affected an animal, accidentally creating a killer virus strain which it could transmit to human beings. Brodie and Shane had thwarted Chinese attempts to manufacture the rogue virus and rendered it harmless. Brought back to Hunza sick and wounded, Brodie had quit his SIS job and decided to stay in the valley. Shane nursed him, fell in love with him and set up house with him to do their research work and look after Hunza people who had no doctor of their own.

All the rest of that day, they toiled though gorges so deep that sunlight rarely penetrated, so dangerous that no-one dared ride a pony. Twice, scree falls forced them to make long detours that lost them several hours. Not until late afternoon did they arrive at the Pasu rest-house; there they put up for the night with the mammoth Pasu glacier tumbling in billows of soiled ice almost to their back door.

Three hours before dawn they resumed their march, knowing that once the sun struck the glaciers they could spend hours slithering over them and risk losing one or two of their ponies with broken limbs. By noon, they had turned left out of the Hunza gorges to trudge along an even bleaker canyon carved out by the Chapursan River; now they had to cross torrents, bled by the sun out of the glaciers high above them. At seven o'clock, they dragged their ponies on to a plateau above the river and sought shelter in a nullah behind a pile of glacier moraine. They had to use these rocks to peg their windbreak and ballast their two tents against the razor-sharp gale that funnelled along the valley from the Hindu Kush mountains at their back. Shigo fed the ponies and built a fire with scrub to heat them and their evening meal. While they ate lamb stew, chupattis and curried vegetables out of mess-tins, they watched a chromatic sunset over the black crags of the Karakorams and the snowline of the Pamirs which crossed the Sino-Russian frontier to the north.

Shane unrolled her sleeping-bag outside the nylon tent and crawled inside without undressing. She lay, observing Shigo build them a stone windbreak, amazed that he wore light clothing against the bitter wind and his woollen Hunza bonnet with the silver ibex badge of his old regiment, the Gilgit Scouts. Brodie was bedding the ponies and checking their tethers. Shane fell to wondering what a research microbiologist was doing in this lonely world. Two and a half years ago, she would have scoffed at anyone predicting she would settle in the Hunza Valley; just as she would have laughed at the thought of falling in love with Paul Brodie with his patched, knocked-about face and the slight limp he contrived to disguise. At first they had fought. Mongoose and snake, as Shigo had said. But then she knew nothing about him; and even after two years she was still discovering bits of his remarkable background. Brodie finished his chores, banked their fire, then pulled her into the tent out of the wind. She zipped open her sleeping-bag, whispering, "Paul, it's warm in here." He slipped in beside her and they went to sleep in each other's arms.

Next day, they left Ikhbal Khan in his own village, judging it too dangerous to expose him to whatever infection had hit Runghar. Four miles further on, as they broke free of the gorge, they sighted the stricken village; it lay in a small oasis shut in by high mountains which were cut by glacier streams feeding the Chapursan River; at this point, the river had spread and divided into several small lakes separated by flat islets of shingle and silt.

Runghar had fifty families living off what they grew in their fields and orchards and from the milk and meat of their sheep and goat herds. Several hundred yards from the first house, a shepherd stopped them until Shigo explained they were bringing medical supplies. Apart from several pi-dogs who came yapping at their heels, nothing stirred in the village. They made for the house of the lambardar—the headman. Like most houses in these valleys, it consisted of four drystone walls covered with mud, divided by partitions inside and with roof holes to admit light and let out smoke. Both the headman and his wife lay on mud ledges that served as beds, covered with goat-hair blankets. Next door, their two daughters were also in bed, ill.

Shane examined the headman and his wife while Shigo translated her questions. Everyone in his village had fallen ill within one or two days, the headman said. Shane turned her head to whisper to Brodie, "I hope you've had shingles."

"Chicken-pox," Brodie replied. "It's the same virus, isn't it?"

She nodded, then parted the headman's woollen shirt to reveal the characteristic belt of blistering along the rib spaces, though on only one side. She palpated the spleen, enlarged like the lymph glands under the armpits. As she worked, the headman explained the illness had started seven days ago.

"But I don't remember ever reading about a single case of shingles or chicken-pox in these valleys," Brodie murmured.

"They mightn't have recorded them."

"This has knocked over about two hundred people," Brodie insisted. "Is shingles so sudden and so infectious?"

"I didn't think so," Shane mused. "Yet, I suppose it can be, especially in an isolated place like this where no natural immunity has developed." She explained the virus of shingles or herpes zoster and the virus of chicken-pox or varicella were almost identical; so children with chicken-pox could infect adults who then went down with shingles; in children, the virus attacked the throat and skin, causing the well-known rash, though no serious effects; however, shingles in adults produced more serious illness since it affected the sensory nerves and often provoked intense pain and sometimes eye trouble and paralysis.

"This old boy has a sore throat as well," Brodie murmured. Shane looked at the lambardar who was pointing at his throat. Shining a pen-torch into his mouth, she noted the tiny vesicles and severe inflammation. "Funny," she said. "The herpes virus and the chicken-pox virus are usually quite specific."

"What I'd like to know is how they got here."

Shane looked at him, a smile crinkling the corners of her grey-blue eyes. "Paul, darling, you'll be telling me next there's been some deep, dark plot to annihilate the village of Runghar."

"Using your own medical logic, if the whole village has gone down, it means nobody had the virus—so somebody must have imported it."

"A virus can lie low for a thousand years," Shane countered, waving a hand to end the discussion and saying they had work to do. They sent Shigo with the ponies to make camp in a clump of trees by the river beyond the last Runghar house since they would need to sleep here that night. During the rest of that day, Shane and Brodie visited every house. Only one old man had died, though probably from exposure because he lived alone and could not rise to feed himself and keep his small fire going. Several houses yielded surprises; it seemed the Runghar virus affected people in different ways; among old people, it appeared to have caused shingles and chicken-pox in equal numbers; several elderly people had fever and lung congestion and two had temporary limb paralysis.

"It could be a new virus," Brodie suggested.

"Not necessarily," Shane said. "Flu can run wild and cause paralysis and encephalitis. This could be a slight change in the shingles and chicken-pox virus. Maybe a mutation."

They could do little for those adults with a mixture of shingles and chicken-pox, or for the children. Having no cortisone ointment to treat the pustules and rashes, they unloaded boric acid powder and lotions on the headman with instructions about how his villagers should use them; against the pain of shingles, they could only prescribe codeine and aspirin and leave small supplies of these drugs for the worst cases. They decided to stay one more day to help the villagers make food and teach those who were recovering how to nurse the others. As they left the lambardar's house, Brodie put a question in Urdu to which the headman replied with a negative gesture.

"What was that about?" Shane asked.

"I asked if he'd had any visitors from over the frontier and he said no."

Shane laughed. "You've still got your cloak-and-dagger mentality," she said as she led the way along the river to their camp. Shigo had placed them the other side of a stream amid a stand of willows and chinars and had already rigged up their two tents. When he had watered and fed the ponies, he cooked them curried vegetables to go with their tins of stewed meat; they ate Hunza apricots and peaches with goatmilk yoghurt and finished with tea which they drank Hunza-fashion, boiled with a trace of the vital salt the valley had to import.

They collected enough deadwood to keep a fire going throughout the night knowing that the cold air would soon avalanche off the glaciers under its own weight and freeze the water round them. As they lit their fire, the valley suddenly vibrated to a booming sound which echoed off the high peaks either side. Instinctively, both Shane and Brodie ducked, fearing one of the many avalanches in these mountains. But Shigo, grinning, pointed upwards. There, against the darkening sky, they saw two long and straight blood-red scars like scalpel strokes; they could not make out the Russian

MIGs, only the last sunlight glowing on their contrails as they streaked south-west into Afghanistan. Those tracks and the sonic bang reminded them of the war a few miles away, the other side of the frontier.

"I'll be glad to get back to Hunza," Shane whispered as they lay together in their sleeping-bag.

"Me, too," Brodie said.

II

SOMEONE PLACED A hand over Brodie's mouth and nose and shook his shoulder. Shigo was whispering in his ear, speaking Urdu which Shane would not understand if she overheard. *"Paul-sahib, gora-log ghar men hain."* Brodie squirmed out of the sleeping-bag and followed Shigo through the tent flap. Although the valley lay in darkness, dawn was already tinging the clouds around the mountain summits. He drew on his boots, then his anorak.

"Sipahi hain?" he asked, thinking they must be soldiers. *"Nahin."* Shigo shook his head. *"Panch admi jo shumal se ata nain."*

Brodie reflected. What were five white-skinned civilians doing so early in Runghar? And who were they, if as Shigo said, they had come along the northern valley?

"Go and keep an eye on them, but don't let them see you," he ordered. "In an hour we'll come into the village to continue our work."

When he had gone, Brodie sluiced his face in the green glacier water; he did not bother with his two-day beard, though realizing that unshaven he looked peculiar since the plastic surgery patches on his right cheek did not grow hair. He brewed tea and toasted several thin chupattis over their gas stove before waking Shane. "We have company," he said, transmitting what Shigo had told him.

"Maybe the lambardar managed to send somebody across the frontier for help," she suggested as they ate the unleavened pancakes with Hunza honey and drank the salty tea. Brodie thought not. When Shane had washed, daylight was filling the valley and they got their medical gear together. As they prepared to set out, she pointed down the river. A man was walking along the bank in their direction; he had not seen them because of the trees shielding their tents and animals. Brodie studied him through field-glasses. He wore a battered cotton hat, a quilted anorak and trousers thrust into calf-length leather boots. From his shoulder dangled a game-bag. He walked slowly, examining the river and the shingle on both banks as though searching for something. Bending down, he picked up a small object and put this in his bag.

When Brodie and Shane emerged from the trees, the man spotted them, training field-glasses on them. "Don't give your name," Brodie said as the stranger quickened his march towards them. "Let him do the talking." On his approach, they took him for thirtyish; he removed his hat to show a thatch of sandy hair; his grey-green eyes appraised first Shane, then Brodie. He held a hand out and they both shook it.

"Dr Josef Dettwiler," he said. "You are here for the sickness?" He spoke English with a thick accent.

"We've come from Gilgit," Brodie lied. He wondered if this man with the good Swiss-German name spoke Schweizerdeutsch. "Where are you from?" he asked.

"The other side of the mountain. We have a Swiss Red Cross team of volunteers helping with the war casualties and we heard about this village. Since when are you arriving?"

"We got here yesterday morning," Shane said. "There wasn't much we could do."

Dettwiler fell into step with them as they headed for the village. "I have three orderlies—two Swedish men and a Hungarian—and we have medicines."

"What do you think has hit the village?"

"That is easy," Dettwiler replied. "Herpes zoster—what in English you call shingles—and varicella—what you call chicken-pox. My men are administering aureomycin subcutaneously to the worst cases. We have hydrocortisone for the skin lesions." He turned and smiled at them. "You are qualified doctors?"

"I am," Shane replied. "My companion is a skilled medical worker."

"If I may ask, how are you finding out about the disease?"

"A village headman went to Pasu and phoned Gilgit," Brodie put in. "It took us four days to get here," he lied.

Outside the lambardar's house, four horses stood tethered. Brodie scrutinized them. Afghans took as much care of their horses as themselves, but these horses had army stamped all over them, and even branded on their hooves. Shigo had said "*panch*". Where was the fifth man? Posted on the northern gorge entrance looking out for anyone appearing from the Hunza side? Dettwiler took them into several houses to watch his orderlies who certainly knew their job, for they were using collodion and benzoin tincture on the blisters and leaving aureomycin capsules with a note on their dosage. To Brodie, it seemed they had come equipped with the right medicines. "Have you seen anything like this elsewhere?" he asked.

Dettwiler flicked him a strange look then shrugged. "It is not unusual in these isolated valleys for a virus to do this," he replied. "There is no fatality."

He issued them drugs to share the task of treating the villagers. Brodie sought out Shigo and sent him back to the camp to await their return. Just before midday, Dettwiler said they had done everything they could; his orderlies had made coffee and fried eggs. Did the English doctor and her companion wish to partake of their meal? For both of them, it turned out to be a nostalgic feast, for the ration packs contained tins of English bacon, plum pudding and bars of Fry's chocolate, a luxury they had not seen for months in Hunza. Brodie noticed the ration boxes bore the Red Cross stencil. Both Swedish orderlies spoke pidgin English but said little while the Hungarian did not utter once. When they had packed their saddlebags, Dettwiler shook their hands and wished them *bon voyage*. "I shall notify the authorities on the other side," he said before leading his contingent towards the gorge heading up into the Irshad Pass and Afghanistan.

Brodie gazed after them then looked at Shane. "Russians," he muttered.

"Paul, your old phobia about the Red menace is showing," she chided.

"That Red Cross story about treating war casualties was got up in case they ran into a Pakistani patrol," he insisted.

"Why risk an international incident to treat sick villagers?" she asked, pertinently.

"Because they knew what they'd find here," Brodie said. "They've obviously seen this type of shingles before."

"I have, too."

He shook his head. "They came over because they've done something to provoke this outbreak." He pointed to the retreating horsemen, then beyond them. "Over there, the Russians have been using napalm and mycotoxins and other poisons—and those chemicals might have modified the virus that struck this village."

"If you go on like this, you'll convince yourself, Paul," she said. "Even if you were right, you'd never prove it."

"I wonder what that phony doctor, Dettwiler, was trying to prove," Brodie mused. "What was he looking for along the river bank?"

They returned along that bank peering at every yard but finding nothing that might have borne the shingles or chicken-pox virus. At their camp, Shigo was waiting for them; he had climbed the hill overlooking the northern gorge. "They had four sentinels in the gorge, Paul-sahib," he said. "All white men." The Hunza had another piece of information that intrigued Brodie even more. "They are taking blood and skin from people in glass tubes," he said.

"So, they're not sure what it is," Brodie remarked.

Shane shook her head. "Nothing more than a routine virus check."

Unconvinced, Brodie had Shigo lead them to the house where the orderlies had collected their samples. With a little persuasion, the farmer and his wife allowed them to draw off blood samples and take several swabs of virus pricked from the skin pustules. His test-tubes containing the blood and swabs he packed in crushed ice in their medical box to keep the virus alive during their return trip. Shane watched without commenting; from living with Brodie for two years, she realized what a determined and thrawn Scotsman he could become when following some idea or hunch like the present one; she also knew that he would have made a brilliant research doctor had a stupid accident not cut his medical studies short when he had all but qualified. Paul had the sort of mind that used a blend of intuition and high intelligence to unravel the most complex situations, and long ago she had ceased to question or doubt it. However, this time she could not imagine what he intended to prove with those virus samples and the infected blood they were carrying back into Hunza.

III

WHEN SHANE ENTERED their clinic just after dawn on the morning after their return from Runghar, Brodie was banging away with two fingers on the typewriter left by a 1930 Karakoram expedition. Picking up the first two sheets, she read a detailed report of their two days in the affected village, including their meeting with Dettwiler and his orderlies. "Shigo's going to Gilgit for supplies and I thought you should send this to New Delhi," he explained, ripping the last sheet out of the machine and handing it to her. Shane acted as a consultant on microbiology to the World Health Organization and worked through its South-east Asia Regional Office in the Indian capital. "We don't normally notify shingles or chicken-pox," she murmured. "But I suppose this one is rather unusual." She signed the document and the covering note Brodie typed. In two days, when Shigo arrived at Gilgit, he would send the documents over the hills to Rawalpindi with the regular Dakota flight and there they would mail it to Delhi.

Shane walked over to the hatcher where Brodie had lit the small gas flame and placed three eggs. "Shigo stole them from under a couple of broody hens," he grinned, taking one and holding it against the light. "The chicks have got to the right stage to challenge with the virus."

"You'll find it's shingles," she said, shaking her head, incredulously.

"Then I'll have wasted my own time."

She shrugged, thinking he had to employ his brain on some puzzle or another, then followed him next door to the clinic; this they had set up as a laboratory with some of the equipment Shane had acquired from her first WHO assignment in Hunza; they had a small centrifuge, two powerful microscopes, a gas frig, racks of test-tubes, retorts, chemicals, vaccines and serum. Brodie had already added his virus samples to a culture medium in which it should thrive; this broth he had treated with antibiotics to kill any bacteria that might ruin his experiment. Now, he meant to inject the virus culture into the chick embryo growing inside the egg. If live shingles virus were present, it would destroy some or all of the embryo cells. Shane watched him aspirate some of the virus into a syringe. Using a small drill, he pierced the blunt end of one egg; he injected the virus solution into the sac surrounding the embryo, closed the small hole with sealing wax and replaced the egg in the hatcher.

"Where are you going to get the serum to make the next test?" Shane asked.

"We've both had chicken-pox, haven't we?" Brodie replied. "So, our blood serum should have enough antibodies to neutralize the virus." As he spoke, Brodie was rolling up his shirt sleeve; he handed Shane a syringe and allowed her to slip a rubber cuff round his upper arm. Skilfully, she found a vein with the needle and drew off enough blood to fill a test-tube. Brodie divided the blood between two test-tubes and clipped these on to the centrifuge and set it spinning to separate the blood serum.

"I'll give you some of mine," Shane proposed, and Brodie repeated the procedure. When the serum had been separated, he filtered and stored it in their deep-freeze.

They had to wait forty-eight hours before they could break open the egg to discover if the herpes virus had attacked the embryo. When they studied it, even with the naked eye they could discern the characteristic pock-marks over the sac and the discoloration of the embryo.

"At least you've got the virus," she said.

"But we've got to check if it's really the shingles and chicken-pox virus."

Brodie mixed the serum he had produced with a small quantity of his "seed" virus from the Runghar victims. This he allowed to sit for a day to give the antibodies time to neutralize the virus. He injected the two remaining eggs, one with his own serum-virus mixture, the other with Shane's. Sealing and labelling the eggs, he placed them in the hatcher. "If there's virus contamination of those embryos, you'll have to send another report saying you've found a new virus, or a mutation," he said.

On the morning of the fifth day after their return from Runghar, even Shane rose early and accompanied him to the lab. Swabbing the first egg with disinfectant, Brodie broke the shell and removed enough to reveal the membrane covering the chick foetus. Covering the membrane was an opaque cloud of tiny pock-marks which also appeared on the embryo—unmistakable signs of virus assault. Their second egg showed the same pattern of virus spread.

They stared at each other, wondering just what it all meant. Finally, Shane said, "Paul, I think we've got hold of a new virus."

"It couldn't be just a strain of the old virus—you know, like flu, or polio where there are several types?"

She shook her head. "According to the text-books, the herpes virus doesn't pull tricks like flu. It has stayed stable for thousands of years."

"Then we'd better tell them in the WHO in case the virus gets out of that valley and starts a real epidemic." They both sat down and began to compile a report on their work with the virus, stressing that their elementary equipment did not allow them to make a real assay of the virus, and their serum antibody might also have been too weak to neutralize the herpes virus.

Later that morning, Shigo returned from his four-day trip to Gilgit. Paul-sahib's papers had caught the afternoon flight the day after he left. As they finished lunch on their terrace, they saw Wali, the wazir's seneschal, signal with a hand-mirror from his master's residence; that meant somebody wanted them at the end of the only phone line into Hunza from Gilgit and Wali had told them to ring back in half an hour. "It's about your first report," Shane said.

She was right. A senior WHO official rang from Delhi to tell her they had studied the Runghar findings and one of their epidemiological experts wished to see them. He would meet them in Bombay tomorrow afternoon. "But that's impossible," Shane exclaimed. "It takes two days by pony and jeep to get to the airstrip at Gilgit."

Wali interrupted her to whisper they were sending a helicopter for the mir's (prince's) son that afternoon, and Shane therefore agreed to keep the appointment in Bombay.

"It is Dr Krishnan and he will wait for you at Santa Cruz airport," the official said.

By the time they had scrambled up the steep, flinty path to the old palace and packed their cases, they heard the racket of the helicopter coming through the southern gorges. When he had picked up the mir's son, the pilot put his machine down on the dead ground behind their clinic. Within minutes they had taken off and were trundling along the valley, then flying just above the deep canyons cut by the Hunza River as it traced its way round Rakaposhi and down to Gilgit. From this viewpoint, the Hunza oases looked like so many opal beads strung on a silver thread. At Gilgit they had held the late-afternoon flight for them.

Brodie never knew whether to be scared or awed stiff by the efforts of this dilapidated Dakota to scrape over the Babusar Pass, nearly thirteen thousand feet high, while caught in the turbulence from Nanga Parbat, last of the Himalayas, and two miles above them. However, the trip had its points; out of the starboard window, the westering sun lit the snows of the Hindu Kush and the peaks of the more distant Pamirs; on their port wingtip they had the great, crenellated glaciers of Nanga Parbat, and below them the Indus. Once over the pass, the mountains dropped away into the Indus plain. In an hour, they touched down at Rawalpindi airport. A WHO official had arranged for them to stay in a government rest-house.

For all the rush, they had to kick their heels in the clammy monsoon heat of Bombay airport before an Air India clerk led them to the VIP lounge. A portly little Indian rose to greet them with a nod, announcing himself as Dr Rama Krishnan, deputy-director of epidemiology for the Delhi office. He had a black face, black eyes and a head shaped like a giant avocado pear tapering to the point where he had parted and plastered his hair and broadening at the base so that his jaw and chin made a straight line. "It is sorry I am to bring you all the way from your happy valley," he murmured without a trace of contrition. "'You are Professor Kingslake?"

Shane nodded. She introduced Brodie and the WHO official threw him the sort of look brahmins give untouchables. "He is not a doctor?" he asked, pointedly.

"He knows more medicine than I do," Shane snapped. "Now, what's all the fuss about?"

"We are going to Cochin," Krishnan said, producing airline tickets from a pocket of his immaculate bush jacket.

"What is happening in Cochin?"

"We are getting report of an outbreak of herpes zoster and varicella like your report," Krishnan replied, then added, "Though it is probably exaggerated and signifies as little."

"If you think that about the reports why bother us?"

"Orders, lady. Orders."

On the two-hour flight they found seats well away from Dr Krishnan, the sort of Indian who pretended to despise everything Western yet acted and dressed like some nineteenth-century pukka sahib. Cochin lay near Cape Comorin, most southerly point on the sub-continent. They followed the western coastline, flying between rugged hills and the sea until they sighted a vast area of coconut palms through which blood-red earth outcropped and which was broken by a series of lagoons. Cochin town lay at the entrance to these backwaters.

Someone in Delhi had booked them into the Satyagraha, a small hotel behind the esplanade with its tourist hotels, full at that season. Krishnan did not even give them time to unpack, hustling them to the quayside where a small motor launch waited. They headed inland, east then south, and within minutes had entered a cool, green world, cruising through a maze of islands and long lagoons fringed with thick coconut and banana groves; now and again, a village appeared through the palm trees and they passed several boatloads of tourists photographing the wild life in this natural reserve; several wild elephants splashed in the shallows and they saw a leopard stalking its kill; in the darker reaches they came across flocks of heron fishing on the banks with the smaller egrets scavenging behind them.

Apart from informing them they were heading for the afflicted village, Krishnan had scarcely spoken to them; he stood in the launch bows jabbering in the local dialect to the pilot. Brodie had unearthed a map in the hotel and was charting their course through the waterways. Just north of Alleppey where the lagoon broadened into a large lake, a boom stopped the tourist boats and they noticed police armed with revolvers and lathis (long truncheons) patrolling the bank and the jetty where they tied up. At this point, a palm grove about two miles wide separated the backwaters from the Arabian Sea. "Here we are disembarking," Krishnan called. A young Indian in sweat-stained shirt and denim trousers led them along a track towards the sea; after five hundred yards, they turned left into a village beside a small lagoon; it was no more than twenty houses constructed from palm trunks interwoven with branches and leaves. Krishnan turned to Shane. "I omitted to introduce you." He pointed to their guide. "This is Dr Ramaswami who thought he should let us know about this occurrence."

In halting English, Ramaswami explained how the illness had appeared five days before and within two days had affected three-quarters of the eighty people, men, women and children; in some, it looked like typical shingles, in others, especially children, it took the form of chicken-pox; however, it had some strange features since some old people had a mixed infection of herpes and varicella which caused chest trouble and for this he had used broad-spectrum antibiotics. Brodie and Shane might have been listening to their own account of the Runghar epidemic. Ramaswami ejected the thick bidi (handrolled cigarette) from his mouth, ground it underfoot and led them into the centre of the village.

Most elderly patients had chests patterned with blisters and the children had the usual skin rash. Five people had limb paralysis and one middle-aged woman had died and was now being cremated at the burning ghat outside the village. "It is because of paralysis and the succumbing of almost the whole village that I am making my report," the young doctor explained.

"You did the right thing," Shane said, but Krishnan shrugged; he gave the impression that he was wasting his precious time.

"Of course we are noting in Delhi," he said. "But it is of insignificant importance since shingles is not a serious illness."

Shane pointed to the smoke palling over the burning ghat. "It can be in elderly people," she said. "Anyway, shingles shouldn't affect the whole population."

Krishnan laughed. "These people have no resistance."

"All right, but where does the virus come from?" Shane said, aware she was echoing Brodie's questions at Runghar.

"It is circulating in the blood, waiting for proper conditions to strike," Krishnan replied. "All this poppycock about strange epidemics is a fearful waste of time."

Brodie was examining the stream running from the lake towards the ocean. "This isn't salt water, is it?" he asked.

Dr Ramaswami shook his head. "They drink it," he said.

Walking back through the village, Brodie noticed they had tethered the water buffaloes and tied up the dozen pi-dogs who were yapping their heads off; several pommel-backed Indian cows were wandering free because of their sacred status. None of those looked like carriers of this curious microbe.

"Bang goes your neat little theory about Afghanistan and napalm and nerve gases," Shane said as they were cruising back to Cochin.

"Are shingles and chicken-pox waterborne?"

"No, airborne," she replied. "Though they're nothing like as highly infective as the virus that hit those villagers."

"How did it get there?" he mused. "How has it landed in two villages fifteen hundred miles apart and at an interval of nine days?"

"Some experts think viruses come around like comets," Shane suggested. "Look at polio which went underground for several thousand years and broke surface a century ago in Sweden, then in America."

In Cochin he bought a large-scale map of India, showing air, rail and trunk routes. But no form of transport served the Hunza region and Runghar, nothing connected those two villages and no-one had visited that isolated village near Alleppey in the two weeks before the outbreak.

"We should have advised WHO to do their assay of the virus," Shane suggested.

"Krishnan would have sneered at you."

To avoid him, they found an Indian restaurant where they ate mulligatawny soup so fiery that it stopped even conversation about the mystery virus; however, the curried lamb and a sweet concocted from local coconuts and bananas were as good as Shigo could have cooked. Afterwards, they wandered along the sea-front to a small headland where natives were still fishing using their strange Chinese nets. Like a giant spider, their six pliant bamboo shafts had swung over the sea on a boom to submerge the huge net attached to them. As Brodie and Shane watched, half a dozen natives hauled up the net with a hundredweight of fish in the bottom. Several fish wriggled through the net, only to fall prey to a dozen gulls cruising overhead who suddenly swooped to grab them.

A bunch of tourists were watching the spectacle, some taking pictures. As Brodie turned to look at them, he found himself staring into a camera held by a man who swung it back quickly to the Chinese fishing net. Intrigued, he followed the movement of the thick-set man with straw-blond hair; he stepped back, behind his companions, still with the camera covering most of his face, still snapping pictures. Brodie kept his eye on him until he had to drop his camera and listen to the Indian guide. Even in this twilight, that face triggered something in his memory, taking him back to his days as a secret agent. Soon, a name clicked in his mind: Werner Krahl. Brodie had seen him twice before. Krahl had turned up in Nicosia and later in Athens during the troubles over Cyprus and the downfall of the Greek colonels in the mid-seventies; he was then posing as a correspondent for the official East German party newspaper, *Neues Deutschland*. His second appearance was as a member of an East German trade delegation to Angola. In both cases, he had been acting as a secret agent for the East German

Staatssicherheitsdienst (SSD) which worked closely with the Soviet KGB, often using its undercover men in proxy roles for the Russian secret police. Krahl (if that was really his name) had obviously recognized him. But who had sent him here, and why? His sight-seeing had probably taken in that quarantined area at the end of the lagoon. Brodie observed the small tourist group drift towards their small bus, emblazoned with the name of the Vasco da Gama Hotel. Since the hotel lay no more than a hundred yards away and the bus took a different direction, he assumed they were doing a night tour of the harbour city. Leaving Shane outside, he wandered into the hotel and sought out a receptionist. He was looking for a member of the party that had just gone on the tour, a certain Mr Schmidt.

"Of a Mr Schmidt we are knowing little or nothing," said the receptionist, a coal-black Tamil youth.

Brodie slipped him ten rupees and the youth pushed the list across the desk. It named seven women and five men booked through the Weltreisebüro in Cologne. However, a thirteenth man had joined the party in Bombay four days ago. Krahl had changed his name once more; now he called himself Herr Gottlieb, a Berlin textile importer, presumably taking time off from buying Indian cotton to relax and do some sight-seeing.

"Who were you looking for?" Shane asked.

"An old acquaintance," Brodie replied. His past as an agent of Her Majesty's Secret Intelligence he kept to himself, knowing Shane had no time for undercover work of any kind.

At breakfast next morning, Krishnan handed Shane two airline tickets to Rawalpindi, saying they could seek reimbursement for the remainder of their flight and travel expenses from New Delhi. "As for me, I am proceeding to Trivandrum to do some real epidemiology on a cholera outbreak and have a well-earned respite."

Now, they understood one of the reasons the little man had wasted his time making this trip. He sneered at them. "You can go back to your sleepy hollow in the Himalayas and forget your fine notions about shingles and chicken-pox," he said. When he had paid his bill and thrown his suitcases into a horse-drawn tonga to make for the station, Brodie turned to Shane.

"Who do we know on the epidemiology side in the WHO at Delhi?"

"Nobody. But there's an Irishman called Terry Slattery in the communicable diseases section."

Brodie took the tickets from her. "If you go and pack, I'll barter these for two first-class tickets to Delhi." Catching her astonished look, he said, "We're going to ask them if they've had any more reports of shingles or chicken-pox outbreaks—and if they have, we'd better tell them it may be a new virus."

"Yes, we've a duty to do that."

Brodie also meant to find out why Herr Werner Krahl had suddenly materialized in Cochin—and if a Red Cross doctor called Dettwiler did really exist.

IV

FROM THE MOMENT they stepped into the airport terminal at New Delhi, Brodie sensed someone was shadowing them. Nothing he saw confirmed this suspicion; only his old agent's instinct told him. Several times, elbowing through the teeming streets and bazaars of Old Delhi or strolling in the imposing bits built by the Raj, he turned abruptly or halted to gawp at something, or crossed the street hoping to surprise the people tailing him. But they were too clever. Anyway, who could distinguish one Indian from another in these crowds and in the uniform dress of kurta (long shirt) and lunghi (loose skirt)? He imagined they were using a whole gang; for never once did he spot the same face behind him for any more than a few minutes.

On his own, he would have eluded or confronted the men; but he did not want to scare Shane into quitting the Indian capital, especially when she was enjoying herself. For her various assignments, WHO owed her several hundred pounds in back pay, and for the first time in two years she had shops where she could spend it freely. In Connaught Place, that series of concentric shopping arcades in the middle of New Delhi, she treated herself to several new dresses, shoes, stockings, scarves, hats. In Hunza, she wore little beside a bush shirt and slacks or shorts with an anorak for the cold weather. "This makes me remember I'm a woman," she said, trying on one of the dresses.

"I don't need clothes to remind me," Brodie said.

She did not forget Shigo, buying him a new bush shirt, trousers and suede boots which Brodie protested would make their Hunza friend look more like the mir than the ruler himself.

They might have stayed at the Imperial or Ashoka or another luxury hotel, but Brodie chose an Indian hotel on the fringes of Old Delhi where he would stand less chance of colliding with so-called military attachés and other phony embassy staff who might recognize him from the old days. For similar reasons, he urged Shane not to tackle the WHO directly about the two small epidemics. Every United Nations agency had its crop of experts with the right qualifications and high efficiency but who, nonetheless, had more concern for their own country's interests than, say, world health or famine relief. They were spies. Brodie knew this at first-hand, having once used the WHO as a cover for his own espionage activities.

While sight-seeing and shopping, he was gathering information about the Delhi office. Shane procured a personnel list, including the various government representatives in the regional centre which covered a vast area taking in India, Burma, much of south-east Asia and Indonesia. Two departments interested him: epidemiology, which studied the various epidemics that occurred in the region, and communicable diseases, which dealt with TB, leprosy and parasitic plagues. Epidemiology came under a Sinhalese, Dr Vikram Jayatalaka from Colombo who had trained in England. However, Brodie spotted the name of Dr Boris Andreevich Chebrakov, a Russian epidemiologist seconded from the Kiev institute for medical research. It meant nothing to him except that the Soviet Union had, as usual, planted one of its men in a strategic position. In this same section, he also noted a Hungarian called Eva Vasari, a woman medical statistician from Budapest University, as well as Krishnan, one of the assistant directors. Communicable diseases had a Parsee director, V. J. Babha, but an Irish deputy-director, Terence Slattery, whom Shane knew from having worked with him on a scrub-typhus outbreak in Malaysia.

Slattery lunched with them, well away from the World Health Organization, in a small restaurant near the Kashmir Gate in Old Delhi. Small, with a light, tripping stride, he had a sad leprechaun face and blue eyes under reddish eyebrows. Somehow, his rolling Dublin brogue had survived twelve years of living in Delhi with an Indian wife. He ate Indian-style, pinching chunks of curried lamb, rice, vegetables between morsels of chupatti with his left thumb and forefinger (the hygienic hand for Hindus) and carrying this to his mouth. He drank whisky and soda throughout the meal, a dangerous habit at midday in such torrid heat. From the courtyard where they sat they had a view across to the Red Fort, one of the Mogul glories with its crenellated walls and cupolas; and further along the half-dry bed of the Jumna River they could see the garden and marble slab where they had burned Gandhi after his assassination. Slattery beckoned a waiter. "*Do beer aur ek whisky lao—jaldi,*" he barked. He spoke army Hindustani in curt, imperative phrases. Slattery gulped his whisky-soda, mopped the sweat off his face and neck with a handkerchief, then used it to swot the flies hovering over the food. Shane regarded his brick-red face with its tracery of exploded capillaries and remembered he had the reputation of being a drunk. "I think you'd be better to forget shingles and get back into the cool hills," Slattery sighed. "A couple of weeks and I'll be in Simla on leave."

"We were on our way back," Shane explained. "But we thought these outbreaks were so strange and wondered if there had been any more."

Slattery shook his head. "I'd never even heard of the Cochin outbreak, or the other one at . . . where is it?"

"Runghar—near the Afghan border."

"Of course, there's no reason why I should have heard," Slattery went on. "Shingles and chicken-pox aren't lethal, highly infectious or quarantinable like smallpox, or important epidemic stuff like flu."

"But Terry, this is very infectious," Shane said, describing what they had witnessed in both villages. "It may be a rogue virus."

"Well, maybe Epidemiology should have passed it to us."

"What happens to reports like ours and Ramaswami's?" Brodie asked.

"If they're considered significant, we shove them on the computer to see if they add up to a health threat—or if they make a regional or a global pattern."

"You have your own computer network?"

Slattery looked at him shaking his head. "No, we buy time and space on the National Physical Laboratory computer across the maidan and we log only our own regional stuff. For the really urgent epidemic material we use our radio link with the Geneva headquarters, or telex."

"So our report would probably get lost in the office along the road," Brodie said.

Slattery nodded. "It might just make a line in the weekly bulletin—and who knows, Geneva might have several more like it from other regions like Africa and the Eastern Med?" He plopped two ice cubes into his whisky, gulped it down, ordered another and coffee for them. He lit a cigarette. "I don't see where you go from there," he said.

"What if it were a new virus, or a mutant of the herpes or varicella viruses?" Brodie asked.

"Now that would be a fish of a different kettle," Slattery said. "They'd have to log that and send a full report to Geneva."

Brodie produced the second report they had written after their lab work on the virus and Slattery listened intently to the way in which they had harvested the virus particles and the infected blood and assayed them. When Brodie had finished, he took the report and scanned it with his faded blue eyes. "You're right," he muttered. "We should put this on the file and through the computer and let Geneva know." He folded the three sheets of typescript. "Is this a spare copy?"

Brodie shook his head. He retrieved the papers and put them in his pocket. "Shane and I have a better idea," he said. "We think perhaps she should give a talk to some of your staff about what we found in Runghar and on the Malabar coast. Could you fix it?" When Slattery said he would, willingly, Brodie passed him a single page on which he had blocked in the announcement of a lecture by Dr Shane Kingslake on the appearance of a new or mutant form of herpes zoster and varicella in two Indian villages. "At least it'll help to pay your dress bill," he grinned at Shane.

"You haven't mentioned that interesting work on the virus here," Slattery objected.

"We thought it should be checked in a proper lab before we give it any weight," Brodie replied.

Slattery pocketed the paper, saying he would have it printed in poster form and distributed that afternoon; he had to give three days' notice to obtain the use of a lecture-room and alert staff who might want to attend.

"Just see that one man gets your poster," Brodie said.

"Who's that?"

"Dr Boris Andreevich Chebrakov."

V

THEY HAD EXPECTED no more than half a dozen people to turn up for Shane's talk, but the small conference room had some twenty people from the various WHO divisions in the regional office. Slattery introduced them to various people, starting with his own chief, Dr Babha, and the head of Epidemiology, Dr Jayatalaka, who thanked them for their work at Runghar and their trip to Cochin. Among the audience, Brodie was surprised to see a young Chinese woman whom Slattery introduced as Dr Huang Ch'ing-hua from Shanghai University medical school. She gave a little bob of her jet-black hair and smiled at both of them. Slattery explained she had just joined the regional staff to gain experience in the epidemiology of infectious and communicable diseases.

Dr Chebrakov was much younger than Brodie had expected. Instead of the baggy jackets and flap-bottomed trousers many Russians favoured, he wore a well-tailored linen suit, a white shirt and red tie. He had flat features, a thin moustache and tartar eyes that travelled carefully over Brodie's patched face as though he were filing it away, mentally. Turning to Shane, he addressed her in clipped but excellent English. "I had no idea you were so young and beautiful, madam," he said.

"I didn't even know you knew my name."

"You are Professor Kingslake who did so much work on the flu virus in the fifties and sixties, are you not?"

Shane laughed. "I'm not as old as all that," she exclaimed. "He was my husband until he died just over five years ago."

"My humble condolences and apologies, madam," Chebrakov said. Those eyes again fixed on Brodie. "I did not catch the name of your collaborator," he murmured. "Dr . . . ?"

"Plain Mr Brodie," Brodie put in.

"He did most of our research," Shane said. "I only have to do the talking."

"And what are you going to reveal about these outbreaks of . . . shingles, isn't it?"

"Haven't you had our first report?" Shane asked.

"Sorry, I must have been away in the field when it came in and my staff failed to draw my attention to your findings," Chebrakov replied. "At present, we have much cholera in the south and the usual pockets of malaria, typhus, the dysenteries and so on." Chebrakov's hint came over clearly: why should he or his department bother with a couple of harmless outbreaks of shingles and chicken-pox? But he also answered one of Brodie's questions: why the Russian had not "lost" their report and the Cochin one and blocked their trip to the lagoons.

"Well, I'm pleased and flattered you could spare the time this evening," Shane said, pointedly.

As she gave her talk, Brodie was observing the audience. While most people merely listened, Dr Huang never stopped scribbling notes, covering pages with ideograms as if determined not to miss one word. However, as Shane outlined the lab work they had done in Hunza on the virus, he saw Chebrakov produce a notebook and a ballpoint pen and take several notes. Two other members of the meeting followed his lead. When Shane had finished her exposition and asked for questions, Dr Huang stood up. "Mode of transmission of this sickness, please?" she said in her tinkling English.

"I wish we knew," Shane replied. "These two outbreaks are a complete mystery and we have thought of everything from lice, fleas, mosquitoes and every form of parasite in animal or insect, we have considered dogs, cats, rodents, everything in the epidemiologist's book. However, of one thing we are fairly certain—the virus does not only spread by airborne infection like the classic herpes zoster or varicella, but may contaminate drinking water. Therefore, we think it may thrive in the gut and be excreted and thus spread."

Chebrakov stood up. "You talk, Dr Kingslake, as if convinced you have discovered a new virus or a mutant virus," he said. "But surely this virus behaves clinically like the shingles and chickenpox virus, and you must admit that your methods of isolating and assaying this virus were crude, to put it at its mildest."

"I agree," Shane said. "Which is why I suggest obtaining virus from the Cochin victims and confirming or refuting our results in your own laboratories which have much better equipment and more experienced staff."

"I think Chebrakov overlooks the fact that this virus seems much more infectious and has a shorter incubation time than either herpes zoster or varicella," Dr Babha interjected. "I think we must follow up this splendid work of Dr Kingslake and Mr Brodie." Other people echoed his opinion. When they seemed to have finished their discussion and run out of questions, he rose and thanked Shane and Brodie for their work and her lecture, and the meeting broke up.

After chatting to various WHO staff members, Shane and Brodie took a tonga back to their hotel to have a shower and change before going to dinner in one of the old-town restaurants. They were preparing to leave when someone knocked at their door. Outside stood a pretty, ash-blonde woman dressed in a printed cotton frock with chaplis on her feet. "I am Dr Vasari," she said. Brodie drew her inside and sat her down. "I have followed your work, doctor," she said to Shane. "Tonight, I heard your lecture and I wondered why you did not mention the outbreak at Riswana."

"Riswana—I know nothing about an outbreak there," Shane said.

"Where is Riswana?" Brodie asked.

"It is a village one hundred and fifty miles from here—just west of Jaipur."

"Tell us about this outbreak," Shane said.

Dr Vasari said that as the medical statistician she had perused the report not long after it had arrived from Riswana about ten days ago; she could not overlook it since she had already read their report on Runghar and the symptomatology was almost identical. A certain Dr Prasad had treated the illness which had affected more than half the population—just over one hundred—in the village.

"This was before the Cochin outbreak?" Brodie queried and the Hungarian doctor nodded.

"We had better have a look at what Prasad says," Brodie declared.

"You will not find it," Eva Vasari said. She explained that when the lecture finished, she wondered why they had not mentioned Riswana, so she went to medical records to search for the file. It had gone. "And yet I placed it there myself with the Runghar and Cochin reports," she said.

"Are they still there?" Brodie asked. She shook her head. "Then perhaps somebody has borrowed them or they've been put on the computer or microfilm."

"I checked all those possibilities," Dr Vasari said. "Anyone borrowing papers must give a signature and they are not microfilmed. I could not check the computer which is only open during the day and I do not know the code in any case."

"What do you think has happened to the reports?" Shane asked.

"I cannot think," the Hungarian replied.

Brodie produced a road map and she pointed out Riswana. They had a good road to Jaipur, then unmetalled roads to the village, she said. If they wished to go, she would lend them her car. Brodie leapt at the offer, and Dr Vasari escorted them to the Mini Minor and handed them the keys. They dropped her at her flat in one of the new suburbs of Delhi. As they drove back to their hotel, Shane turned to him. "What do you think has happened to the reports?" she said.

"I'd say Chebrakov has borrowed them and just forgot to sign for them or to put them back." He grinned at her. "Funny, he didn't strike me as an absent-minded type."

VI

BRODIE HAD DECIDED to make the four-hour drive between midnight and four o'clock to avoid the great heat during the day in that part of the Indian plain, and the bullock carts and other traffic on the roads. At that time, on the main trunk road to Jaipur, they met hardly anything in the way of cars. However, when Shane had gone to sleep in the back of their car, Brodie stopped twice to make sure no-one was following them. At four o'clock, ten miles west of Jaipur, he drew off the road into the shade of some willows by a stream and brewed tea for both of them. Since they now had to travel over rutted tracks left by carts, they waited for dawn before continuing. It still took another two hours to reach the village because they heeded peasants' directions.

Riswana sat by the edge of a small, freshwater lake fed and emptied by two sluggish streams. It was a huddle of mud or lath-and-plaster houses surrounding a village square with some stone buildings and a whitewashed Hindu temple. At that early hour, some villagers were moving the charpoys (string beds) on which they had slept in the open; a dozen children ran to jump on their car, probably never having seen its like in their village. Soon, the village headman arrived with the local brahmin priest and schoolmaster to greet them, Hindu-fashion, with hands clasped before their mouths. Brodie explained in Hindustani why they had come. At that, the headman declared they must convene the *panchayat* or village council. Within minutes half the village, men, women and children, had gathered round the well in the square to listen to the white man's questions in his strange accent and their own councils' replies; they shouted interjections themselves.

It was true, their village had been smitten by this curious sickness which not even its oldest inhabitant had encountered. This happened fourteen days ago, and the sickness lasted one week, although some people still suffered severe pain from it even now. Again, Brodie and Shane felt they could have been hearing the lambardar at Runghar or Dr Ramaswami in Cochin, so closely did all the accounts tally.

"Why the interest of the gora-log in this sickness?" the headman asked.

"Have other white men been here, then?" Brodie asked.

"Ji-han," said the headman, nodding. "One white man who came with the doctor. A tall, fair man with eastern eyes and a moustache." Brodie and Shane gazed at each other, both thinking that Chebrakov had taken time away from his cholera studies to come here and see the shingles outbreak himself.

"Did the villagers notice anything unusual in the days before the sickness?" Brodie asked. "A strange man or woman?" Their heads shook in unison. "Anything dead, then? A rat, a dog, a bullock?"

One man had seen a hyena go through the village at night; another had come across a dead bandicoot rat, though in the fields. Brodie did not ask about mosquitoes; everyone had those. He told the villagers to reflect about anything else that might have caused the sickness while he and Shane strolled round the place. Riswana lay about fifty yards from the lake and slightly above it.

"Funny," he remarked. "There's always water."

"Dettwiler was searching for something along the river," Shane prompted. "What for, I wonder."

Brodie pointed to the lake. "They can't drink this," he said, dubiously.

"No, but being Hindus, they'll all bathe in it."

While strolling along the lake edge, they scrutinized the swampy ground between the water and the tangle of couch grass and scrub. "There are fish, anyway," Shane murmured, pointing to the ripple as a fly-catching fish broke the smooth surface.

"And cats," Brodie said, picking up the bone of a small fish with head and tail intact.

"A cat would never survive in a village with two dozen pi-dogs after it," Shane scoffed. "And no Indian cat would leave the head and a bit of the tail. It must be something else—perhaps a cormorant or some other bird."

No sooner had she uttered the word than Brodie stopped in his tracks. "Shane, you've got it—birds, that's what could carry the disease." Mentally, he began to compute the time lapse between the Runghar outbreak, this one and Cochin. "It was seventeen days ago they had the first cases in Runghar," he mused. "And three days later it hits this village, and eight days after that the Cochin backwater." Turning, he strode back to the village with Shane jogging to keep abreast of him.

Again, they had to wait for the panchayat to convene and another crowd to collect before he could begin his interrogation. Had anyone seen a strange bird around the lake just before the sickness happened? His question rippled through the crowd, being passed from mouth to mouth. One man raised his hand; he wore a blue cotton shirt over a breech clout and his grizzled face was capped by an orange bonnet. He was jabbering too fast for Brodie to follow, and the schoolmaster translated.

"Asari is fisherman and two strange fishing birds is seeing at twilight by the stream and lake."

"What kind of birds?"

Asari mumbled and the schoolmaster said, "Of their kind, Asari is unsure, but such birds with two tails on Sambhar Lake he is once seeing."

"Where is that?"

"Jaipur-way."

"Can he describe these birds?"

"Is twilight and of their colour he cannot speak. But this he is saying—he is watching the birds because they are looking and behaving as one bird, they are fishing and flying away as one."

"They are big?"

Asari pointed upwards at the kite-hawks planing overhead. With his scrawny hand, he made a swooping motion, muttering something that sent a gust of amusement through the crowd. "The birds with better fortune are fishing than Asari," the schoolmaster translated.

"Did they make a sound?"

Nodding his head, the old fisherman opened his gap-toothed mouth and made a croaking then a cawing sound—like a crow. A burst of applause and laughter ran through the crowd.

"Which way did they fly, the birds?"

Asari had no doubt about that; he turned and pointed both arms south. Obviously revelling in his notoriety, he led them willingly to the spot where he had observed the birds and acted out with exaggerated gestures the way they had hovered, low above the water, waiting their chance before pouncing on the fish and how they ate on the wing or stripped their catch clean on the bank.

"Is the sahib believing the sickness comes with these birds?" the headman asked.

"Perhaps with this one type of bird," Brodie replied. "But to kill the birds would increase the danger." He did not want the villagers to begin exterminating bird life in their area.

They had a job to escape from the village, for not every day did a white sahib and mem-sahib drive a petrol-gari into Riswana. They drank tea so sweet they could have stood a spoon in it, and ate sticky rice-cakes and heard fifty different tales of how the sickness had affected various villagers. It was eleven o'clock when they drove back along the cart track to join the Jaipur road. At that hour before midday, the heat, the glare, the long night's drive and their long session in the village had begun to tell on both of them. In Jaipur they found a rest-house and rented a room for the day. Shane peeled off her clothes and stepped under a cold shower to wash the dust off herself while Brodie lay down under the whirling punkah in the centre of the ceiling. "Paul," Shane called. "I've always longed to spend a day in the pink city of Jaipur and look at the Palace of Winds and the Jantar Mantar observatory—and all I want to do is sleep." Brodie did not answer. When she came back into the bedroom he was lying flat-out, fully-dressed on the mattress of the string-bed, dead to the world.

VII

WHEN SHANE WOKE, the sun was slanting through the rush-matting blinds in the rest-house. Her watch read seven o'clock. She saw Brodie had placed a jug of *nimbu pani* by her bedside and she drank some of the natural lime juice; he had also done some shopping, for a couple of books lay on the table of the spartan room with his large-scale maps; and he had bought bottled water for their trip back. As she finished sluicing her face with water, Brodie entered carrying bread rolls, yoghourt and a wedge of the almond cake she liked. "I've bought a chicken and given it to them to cook tundoori-style," he said.

Shane went to pick up the books, both second-hand, one bearing the stamp of a British Army library from the Second World War. He had unearthed *The World of Birds* which dated from the thirties, one of those picture books with short captions on each species; his second find, the American edition of *A Field Guide to the Birds of Britain and Europe* by Peterson, Mountfort and Hollom, published in the fifties. "Well, have you come across Asari's white crow that fishes in Indian lakes and hunts in pairs?" she said, smiling.

"You don't believe the bird theory then?"

"No—I just don't see this strange bird, or any other bird, infecting people with shingles or chicken-pox."

"But birds do carry viruses that attack human beings."

"I grant that," she replied. "Parrots with psittacosis and pigeons with ornithosis. But they're airborne viruses only transmitted to people in close contact with the birds."

"But say this virus has changed by passage through the birds—say it's become waterborne . . ."

Shane laughed. "That's about as good as your notion of a virus changed by Afghan nerve gas."

"All right, then, the birds have picked up some tick that has learned to carry the chicken-pox virus."

"No, Paul."

Brodie did not reply directly; instead, he unfolded his map and spread it on the table. She noticed he had ringed Runghar and drawn a line through it and through Cochin; this line ran about fifty miles west of Riswana. "My guess is those birds came over the hills from somewhere in the Soviet Union and they flew through something—nerve or mustard gas, nuclear radiation—something that caused a change in the virus they were carrying and they passed it on to the people they contacted along that route."

Shane listened to his argument that the birds had taken three days to fly from the Afghan border to Riswana then another nine days to make their way to Cochin. Didn't that look like a migration route? In reply, Shane handed him his two books. "Read these— they'll tell you birds don't migrate in high summer, either to their breeding grounds or winter quarters. And gulls don't fish a thousand miles inland on Indian lakes." Brodie looked so crestfallen as she demolished his theory that she went, put her arms round him and kissed the smooth, hairless skin on his right cheek. "Let's get back to our valley and forget all this," she murmured.

"But I have a smell about . . ." he started to say, and she placed a hand over his mouth.

"Just tell them at WHO what we've seen and leave it to them," she urged.

"All right," he said, finally.

A knock came at the door and a waiter came in bearing their chicken and half a dozen different types of curried vegetables and several condiments. With him, the restaurant manager entered, wearing a white jacket, white trousers, white shirt and even a bow tie in their honour. "Are you wishing wine, sahib?" he asked.

"Wine—what sort of wine?"

"I am having Scottish whisky wine, or French wine."

"Let's see your French wine," Brodie said, and the man disappeared to return with a bottle of cognac, its label written in both English and Hindi, revealing it had originated in Poona in the

Deccan. Brodie had encountered such firewater before and knew it consisted of a mixture of wood alcohol and laboratory spirits and could knock a man over even in thimblefuls. "And you call that French wine," he grunted.

"Is French-style like I promised. Is brewed from grapes specially imported from south of France."

They burst out laughing. "We'll try it," Shane said, but Brodie waved the bottle away. "Too hard on the optic nerve," he whispered to her. "Methyl alcohol." He ordered the Delhi beer they had drunk during their stay in the capital. The rest-house meal more than compensated for the manager's fantasies; he had spiced and roasted the chicken himself, even cooked the rice with coconut milk and lightly curried the vegetables; as a sweet he had made them his own speciality, pineapple balls.

They kept the room until midnight, deciding to drive back during the cool night hours. When Shane had finished packing, she went to have a shower to cool her down. She emerged from the bathroom to discover Brodie immersed in the larger of the bird books, reading its section on migration and leafing through the pictures looking for Asari's bird. As she often told him, he was just a thrawn Scotsman who wanted to prove everybody else wrong.

VIII

SLATTERY NO MORE believed the bird story than Shane. It ran counter to virus theory and ornithological experience. However, at Brodie's insistence, he photocopied their report on Riswana with a note about birds acting as potential carriers of the disease and distributed this round the regional office recommending various departments to alert their field men about birds if they came across the disease. "When are you going back?" Slattery asked.

"Tomorrow afternoon," Shane replied.

From a cupboard in his office, Slattery produced two bottles of beer. When they refused his drink offer, he still poured himself one. "Wish I were coming with you," he mumbled, gulping the liquor and scavenging its froth with his tongue.

"You'd never get there, Terry," Shane said. "That two-day trek at eight to ten thousand feet would slay you. And in Hunza, you'd have to live mainly on fruit and cereals without your two packets of cigarettes a day and your liquor ration and your nice air-conditioned office."

"Fruit and cereal," he muttered. "In that case, you'd better have a good meal tonight. I'll book us a table at the Raj Mahal in the old town." He immediately called a chuprassi and handed him a note to take to the restaurant, reserving a table for eight o'clock. "You'll have the best Indian meal you've ever tasted," he promised.

Before leaving the WHO office, they called on Dr Vasari to thank her for the car and find out if she had checked the computer records. Her office in Medical Statistics lay empty. She had gone, said her Indian secretary. Yesterday afternoon, the Hungarian consulate had called her. Brodie handed the girl the car keys. "Did she leave any message for us?" he asked.

"Only to say Dr Chebrakov had the files you were seeking," the girl replied. "He told Dr Vasari there was no need to log them with the computer."

Shane called the consulate. An official demanded her name and relationship with Dr Vasari before giving her any information. "She left Delhi last night to return to Hungary on compassionate grounds," he said. "Her father is very sick."

"I thought it might be her grandmother's funeral," Brodie said when Shane relayed the message. "Chebrakov obviously had a word with the Hungarians and that was what Eva Vasari wanted us to know."

"But why do they want to keep these small outbreaks quiet?"

"I wouldn't think even Chebrakov knows the reason for that," Brodie said.

Slattery had put a WHO car at their disposal and they spent a couple of hours sight-seeing before returning to their hotel to pack their belongings ready for the trek back into Hunza the next day.

In the cool evening, they walked the mile to the Raj Mahal restaurant, making a detour through the lawns and gardens round the Jama Masjid, one of the most noble and striking mosques in the east, then through some of its worst slums. As they approached the restaurant, a tonga trotted past them and Slattery hallooed them from its covered interior, halting the two-wheeled buggy to invite them aboard. "I don't trust myself with a car in this part of Delhi," he explained. On reaching the restaurant, Brodie heard him order the driver in his peremptory Urdu to return for them at eleven o'clock and wait outside if they were late.

At the Raj Mahal, they treated Slattery like a sahib. He and his guests were shown to the best table in the deep courtyard from where they could survey the other diners and the evening skyline of Delhi, yet remain fairly private. Slattery had not exaggerated about the meal; two boned chickens had been stuffed with a mixture of finely chopped ham, curried rice, and a mixture of eggs, onions and peppers, then roasted and basted in a primitive pit oven over sandalwood. A bewildering array of curried vegetables succeeded one another on the table, and this was followed by a mouth-watering halva. Brodie noticed that, like most heavy drinkers, Slattery had little appetite; he got through half a bottle of Scotch, then drank rice-wine during the meal. "Your little bit of paper on Riswana caused quite a stir in the office," he said with his wry, leprechaun grin.

"Chebrakov?" Brodie prompted.

"You guessed it." Slattery lit his umpteenth cigarette and refilled his glass. "He put round a memo shooting down what he called your bird-brained theory, implying we'd all be a laughing-stock if we started mixing up epidemiology and ornithology and suggesting birds carried shingles." He gulped another mouthful of rice-wine. "Somebody else got worked up about it," he said. "Our Chinese friend, Dr Huang."

"Did she knock it down?"

"On the contrary, she said she believed it."

"Chebrakov's probably right," Shane said, looking at Brodie, who merely shrugged.

It was nearly midnight and the cummerbunded waiters were putting out the oil lamps in the courtyard when Slattery called for the bill and paid; they made their way through the main restaurant to the waiting tonga. A moon was lighting the cupolas of the Red Fort and the Jama Masjid and glittering in the Jumna River. Slattery pulled down the back step of the tonga and Brodie helped Shane under the hood then climbed up beside her; he hoisted the tiny Irishman into the buggy knowing he would have had difficulty scrambling over the step with the load of liquor he was carrying. "Does he know the road?" he asked.

"Ay," Slattery gasped then snapped a string of Urdu, telling the man to go first to the Nataraj Hotel to drop them, then to his own home. "Jihan," the driver murmured, cracking his whip over the scrawny horse and sending him forward at a slow trot. They crossed the Chandi Chowk bazaar, its stallholders sleeping in their shops or even on charpoys outside to get whatever breeze was blowing; they passed under the railway bridge, heading for the hotel. Slattery's head was lolling and he was snoring while Shane had cradled her head on Brodie's shoulder. He himself felt drowsy after the long day and the heavy meal.

For what seemed a minute or two, he dozed before something alerted him—perhaps the fact they seemed to have slackened speed, or had left the bazaar lights behind them. Brodie sat up and began to take stock of their surroundings. First, they passed an all-night stall lit by carbide lamps which sold groceries, betel nut, bidis; a few hundred yards beyond this lay a small Hindu temple spilling light across the road; but on either side, in the flickering light of their two oil lanterns, he glimpsed nothing but mud-and-lath hovels and a few figures sleeping on charpoys between them and the odd oxen lying in the shafts of their waggons. Now, the horse's hooves were hitting hard earth rather than asphalt, which seemed strange. Brodie went to ask the driver where they were going when he saw the moon behind them. It had been on their left hand when they started. So, they must have turned west. Why? This man wasn't making for the Nataraj Hotel or Slattery's home. Had they switched another man for the driver who had taken them to the restaurant? Was he leading them into an ambush?

As he sat, wondering how to act, they rattled over a level-crossing, lit with a feeble electric lamp. Brodie peered behind them. About a hundred yards back, several shadowy figures flitted through the crossing light. They wore long shirts over dhotis. He counted six at least. They were on foot, trotting behind them, making hardly any sound in the still night. He had no doubt they were Indians. Probably hired dacoits. They'd all wind up garotted or floating down the Jumna with their throats cut and nobody would ever discover who, how or why. On the other side of the tonga, Slattery was snoring his head off. No use trying to wake him or enlist his help; by doing that, he would merely put the driver on his guard.

Brodie put a hand over Shane's mouth and nudged her. He whispered in her ear. "Don't make a sound. We're being followed by a gang of dacoits." Softly, he explained he was going to try to overpower the driver and make a run for it. Without upsetting the trim of the tonga, he changed places with Shane. Now, they had gone beyond the houses and seemed to be travelling over waste ground. Against the dark sky, the driver had become only a blurred silhouette. Brodie had to hit precisely on the right spot, then catch him before he fell and startled the horse. Inching up behind the man, he fixed a spot on the nape of his neck, just below his coiled pagri. With all his force, he brought the edge of his right hand down on the spot; as the man slumped forward, Brodie grabbed him with his left hand and dragged him back into the tonga. "Tie him up with his pagri," he ordered Shane as he clambered on to the driver's perch and grabbed the reins.

In the feeble moonlight, Brodie could distinguish little in the way of landmarks; his lanterns merely lighted a few yards ahead and on either side. But he saw no buildings and guessed the driver had received orders to take them beyond the city limits into a deserted area where their pursuers could quietly murder them. Somehow, he had to turn this old nag round and get back into the town and give at least one or two of them a chance of escaping. Brodie hooked his whip handle through one of the lantern rings and pulled it free of its socket. "Put something over it, but keep it alight," he whispered as he passed it to Shane. He did the same with the second lantern. Brodie waited until she had rigged up a blanket to black out the lights before yanking on the reins and pulling the old horse round in a tight turn. Whipping the animal into a fast trot then into a gallop, he drove straight at the gang pursuing them, surprising and scattering it. But a couple of the men sprinted after them; one caught hold of the horse's bridle and the other held on to the traces to try to stop the animal. Brodie lashed out with his whip at the first man until he let go. To dislodge the man on the traces, he used the butt and cracked him over the head, knocking him senseless. As they jolted back over the level-crossing, Brodie realized this tired and underfed nag would never keep up its pace; already, he was flagging and blowing hard with fatigue and Brodie could hear the shouts of the gang behind as it closed on them. They would not even reach the bazaar at this rate. Brodie turned and yelled at Shane. "Throw the driver out."

In the back, the swaying and shaking had roused Slattery.

Quickly, Shane explained the situation, but it took the fuddled Irishman several moments to grasp what she was meaning. Holding a lantern to the driver's face, he muttered, "But he's nothing like my man."

"Throw him out," Brodie shouted.

Slattery pushed down the back step of the tonga and rolled the driver over it. As he hit the hard earth they heard him bellow with pain. But it did not make much difference to their progress and it did not stop the gang from pursuing them. Now, they were racketing along the narrow slum street. Ahead, Brodie spotted the light from the small temple and beyond that, the all-night stall. To the bazaar and safety, he reckoned another mile and a half. Yet, unless they lightened the load ever further, this blown old hack would never make it. That Hindu store would sell ghee and paraffin oil for lamps. That gave him an idea which might work and might not; however, it was better trying anything than being trapped in a dark alley and carved up by these Indian thugs. He whipped the horse on and called over his shoulder, "Shane, come and take the reins."

"What are you going to do, Paul?"

"I haven't time to explain." He grabbed her arm, pulled her on to the bench and handed her the reins. "See the town lights ahead? Make for them. Slattery will have to take his chance with me."

In the back, he picked up the two lanterns and turned their wicks up full. He shouted a briefing at Slattery, repeating it to get it into his drunken mind. "When I give the word, you must jump and make for the railway. Fifty yards down the line there's a signal box. Alert the railway police and tell them to pick up the tonga with Shane. Got that?" Slattery nodded.

Brodie was watching over Shane's shoulder for the temple. At the precise moment they passed it, he nudged Slattery. "Jump," he ordered. Out went Slattery, hitting the ground rolling over then staggering to the right. At the same time, Brodie backhanded one of the lanterns in a high arc, aiming at the ground in front of the temple. It fell there and, as it shattered, the lamp spilled its oil across the road and this blazed up in the faces of the gang. Brodie hoped it would dazzle them for a few moments and give Slattery the chance to pick himself up and make his escape. A dozen pi-dogs, wakened by the noise and light, came snarling and yapping after the gang.

They had just over two hundred yards to run to the Hindu store and Brodie ticked off the seconds as he watched the thugs skirt the flames and come sprinting after them. This time, he must let them see him dart from the tonga so that he would draw them off and leave Shane a free run. Brodie clutched the lantern by its base; he would have to time the blow to the second and make sure the lamp hit the right target. Over Shane's right shoulder, he glimpsed the store light. As they jolted past it, he leaned out the back of the tonga and tossed the lantern into the centre of the stall. Glass splintered and a long ribbon of flame flared upwards into the roof thatching and streamed through the stall. Brodie saw the stallholder and two of his customers run into the street just as something exploded, showering fire into the road. Within seconds people were gathering round the blazing stall, shouting and trying to douse the flames with dirt.

"Paul, don't jump, stay with me," Shane called.

"We'd never get there," he shouted back. He leapt, hit the ground with both feet and rolled over, then picked himself up and ran for the nearest houses. In that street, lit by the blaze, the gang could not fail to see him. In any case, if he guessed right, they wanted him and not Shane whom they could handle later. He plunged along one of the dark alleys behind the street; there, he had to move cautiously, groping over recumbent bodies and round charpoys. He had hoped to lose himself in that slum maze, but had not reckoned with the pi-dogs which ran, barking and baring their teeth at his heels, waking people and giving him away. Behind him, he heard somebody shout, in Hindi, "Stop the white thief," and he broke into a run. In the dark, he stumbled against bed frames, knocked against people and even a cow which was wandering along the alley. A hundred yards along the alley, he bore left and suddenly found himself back in the street he had quit. To his left, a crowd still surrounded the burning store, but he could see several men who appeared to be searching for him; to his right, fifty yards away, the pool of oil from the broken lamp still guttered outside the temple. Keeping close to the houses, Brodie headed for the temple thinking he might hide there until the gang had called off their hunt for him. Before he entered the temple, he turned and shooed off the pi-dogs.

Outside, it was a low stone-and-stucco building with a cupola in the centre and four ornate pillars around this; inside, it had a sunken, earthen floor with three steps leading to the main place of worship and the statue of the god to whom the temple belonged. Amid offerings of fruit, flowers, vegetables and ghee, an earthenware lamp flared at the feet of the tall statue; its fluid light heightened the expression on his grinning face and played on his four arms, two of which held a flute. He struck a dancing pose. Brodie grimaced. Trust himself to pick a temple to Shiva the Destroyer, most baleful member of the Hindu Trinity. But the ominous figure of Shiva might prove useful, for behind him were a series of pillars supporting the temple cupola and a niche in which he might hide. To make sure there were no priests, Brodie advanced cautiously; but the place appeared deserted. Behind the dancing god, another doorway gave access to the back. He shot home the wooden bars of the door. A short flight of stone steps ascended to the flat roof around the cupola, his funk run if he needed one.

Brodie blew out the light and felt his way behind the statue. If they came and discovered him, at least he had something to put his back against and he might stop one or two of them from the top of the stairs. With his back resting against two of the god's four legs, he prayed Shiva the Destroyer was having a night off. In the airless building, the heat was stifling; his exertions and the emotions of that night had left him breathless and sweating; a smell of ghee and rancid oil made his nostrils curl and cut his breath. He would have given much for even a lathi with which to defend himself.

He lay there for an hour and a half before they found him; they must have searched all round then perhaps followed the pi-dogs which still hung around the temple, barking. Brodie heard someone trying the back door. Then a dog yelped and the barking receded. That way, he knew they were coming. Peering at the entrance, he could just discern one shape after another entering the temple. He lay quite still, hoping they would not look too hard. But they fanned out, cleverly, posting two of their number at the door before moving round and starting their search with flashlights. They seemed no ordinary dacoits, though Brodie saw that each carried the traditional dacoit dagger. Let them get behind him and he would have no chance at all. He waited until one of them had almost stumbled over him before making his move. Getting to his feet, he grabbed the Indian by the arm, twisting it and wresting the dagger from it. Hearing the scuffle, the others closed in; but Brodie was already moving back, keeping the dagger pressed against the Indian's back and using him as a shield.

He took the only escape route—up the stairs to the roof. Once there, he might jump and bolt for it. With the dacoit in front of him, he went back up the stairs, one at a time. Several torches shone in his face, blinding him, but no-one could pass him on the narrow stairs. Near the top, Brodie suddenly thrust the Indian down on top of the others and as they tangled in a heap at the bottom of the steps, he turned and dashed out on to the roof.

But he never reached the low parapet. A dozen hands grabbed him. He started to struggle and free himself but something seemed to detonate at the nape of his neck and he went down, senseless, at their feet.

IX

WITH NOTHING BUT her own weight on the tonga, Shane whipped the horse into a fast trot and soon outdistanced the few men who still pursued her. Ten minutes after Brodie had bailed out, she cantered into Sadar Bazar street and turned the tonga towards the main railway station where she left the vehicle. From previous visits to Delhi, she knew where police headquarters lay, near the Jumna. There, she explained what had happened to a desk sergeant who produced several forms and was starting to interrogate her when she halted him, knowing what Indian bureaucracy was. "Two men will be dead if you don't do something quick," she snapped. "And one of them is a high-placed international civil servant working for the World Health Organization."

That stirred him to action and, at her suggestion, he phoned the railway police. Yes, they had a report of a fire in the Lok district. And an Englishman had come into a signal box to say he and his friends had been attacked by dacoits. "Ask if he is hurt," Shane said.

"No, only one ankle injury, they are saying."

Shane shook her head. "Why does He protect drunks?" she mused. To the sergeant, she said, "Now you know it's serious can you tell one of your police cars?"

"You are showing them?"

Shane nodded. She had to wait an eternal half-hour before he located a car and a crew of three armed policemen; she directed them back along the road she had taken. When they reached the store, a fire still smouldered and a crowd stood around the gutted stall. But no-one had seen either thugs or a white man at the time the fire started. As the police were finishing their interrogation of the stall-holders and witnesses, a brahmin priest approached and pointed to his temple, requesting the police to follow him. "They are defiling Shiva's temple by murder," he protested, and one of the policemen translated this for Shane who shivered as she walked behind them, thinking they had caught and killed Paul.

When they entered the temple, the priest lit several oil lamps and led them behind the statue of Shiva, the dancing god, to the stairs. There, across the bottom step lay an Indian with a stab wound in his upper abdomen. Blood had pooled and was coagulating beneath him showing he had received his wound recently. "Mar Ghia," (He is dead) the priest murmured.

Shane gazed at the dead man. He had a young face, darker than a northern Indian's, as though he came from the southern provinces of Madras or Kerala. "Is more blood on stairs and roof," said the priest, leading them upwards. In their torchlight, the police noted several large blood-stains on the steps and near the roof parapet.

"Did you see or hear any of this fighting?"

"Nothing," the priest said. Nor had he touched anything.

"Did you see anything of a white man?" Shane asked, but again the brahmin shook his head. She realized that, even if this man or any natives in the district had witnessed the fight, they would never disclose the fact since none of them wanted anything to do with the police. On the dead man, the sergeant discovered no clue to his identity, and Shane could guess they would carry out no forensic tests before they burned him. Not even a post-mortem. They had classified it as a dacoit murder, something that happened too frequently in Delhi Territory or Uttar Pradesh state. Such men, if they had not already killed Paul, would demand a fortune in ransom money, and even after receiving it, might murder him.

When she returned to police headquarters, Slattery was waiting there for them, and added to her fears. They had summoned him to identify the tonga driver, who had just been discovered on waste ground near the Raj Mahal restaurant with his throat cut. "They must have followed us to the restaurant then killed the driver and put one of their own men in his place," the Irishman said.

Shane gazed at him. "But that must mean they had planned to murder us, so they're not dacoits."

"They might just be thugs hanging around restaurants on the lookout for Europeans," Slattery said with a shrug.

Shane did not agree. She was now beginning to suspect that the attempt on them had some connection with those epidemics. Paul had not told her everything he thought about those mysterious outbreaks, but she knew he felt there was some dark plot behind them and somehow Chebrakov and the Russians were involved. She revealed nothing of her suspicions to Slattery, fearing he might gossip in the WHO office. Her first job was to find Paul if he were still alive; if they had killed him, she would avenge his death. Yet, where did one start in this city of a million souls and a maze of thousands of slums where even the police ventured warily? What would Paul have done had she disappeared?

First, she bullied the police into beginning a hunt for Paul and went with them while they questioned everyone in and around the restaurant who might have witnessed the attack on the tonga driver, or any of the gang which pursued the buggy. Then, in the heat of the day, she herself took a taxi into the slum area with Slattery to help interpret for her. They searched the temple for clues and verified that Paul had hidden there, for on the stairs they came across one of the leather buttons he had been wearing on his bush shirt that evening. When they had sought out the priest, Slattery with his barrack-room Hindustani scared him into believing the police suspected he had collaborated with the thugs to kill and rob a white man. He shook his head, covered with ash and white paste. But Slattery kept on, and eventually the man went to a corner of the temple and, from behind an effigy of Kali, wife of Shiva, he produced one of the chaplis that Brodie had worn. With this information, they went back to the police who issued the press with a description of Brodie and the circumstances of his disappearance.

Shane also went to the British High Commissioner's office where a security officer, a former Guards sergeant-major, listened to her story. "Did he have money?" he asked.

"A couple of hundred rupees, that's all."

"Still more than enough for a gang of thugs to rob him and cut his throat," the man said, consolingly.

Footsore, weary and depressed, Shane returned to the Nataraj Hotel that evening, having tramped round half a dozen police stations, questioned the railway police at the main station and enlisted the help of newspaper correspondents. She ordered a light meal in her room and was finishing this when her phone rang. A sing-song Indian voice said, "Do not speak, only listen. Your friend is alive. If you wish to see him, present yourself at Ashoka Pillar at six o'clock precisely. Do not tell anyone, do you hear? No-one. Especially police. Make sure you are not followed. Take three taxis in different directions. If you are followed you will never see him again. Understood?"

"Understood," Shane repeated. She replaced the phone. Paul was alive! A prisoner, but alive! And if she went to the rendezvous tomorrow night she might join him in captivity. However, she did not even consider failing to keep the appointment. Had not Paul saved her life twice? And risked his own life last night? Judging from the blood spilled in that temple, he might be wounded.

Next day, she did not venture out, thinking Paul's captors might be watching her and imagining she was contacting people and therefore kill him. In the evening, she obeyed instructions, picking up a taxi outside her hotel, dropping it and finding another at Connaught Place, then a third to the law courts from where she walked to the Ashoka Pillar. She realized why they had chosen this landmark, more than two thousand years old, where British and loyal Indian troops held out against a huge native force during the Indian Mutiny; at that hour, tourists were thronging the base of the monument to take pictures and listen to its history.

"I am guide if you are wishing, Kingslake mem-sahib," someone whispered and she turned to see an Indian in a white Nehru cap, white tunic and European trousers. On his chest, he wore an official guide's badge. Shane nodded, then pretended to listen as they strolled round the stone column detailing its story. As they approached Ridge Road, he murmured, "There is red Fiat taxi by

Mutiny Memorial. You will hire this. Now, give me ten rupees." Shane paid him, then walked left, her legs shaking with apprehension. A red cab moved away from the kerb and she flagged it to a halt. Someone opened the back door and she got in. To her surprise, she saw a native in a well-cut linen suit, white shirt and a green silk tie. He had a face resembling Shigo's with lightly-bronzed skin and slate-grey eyes that fixed on her face, intently but impersonally, before he turned to peer through the rear window at a car moving away from the kerbside at their pace. "It is one of ours," he said without turning the W sound into a V like most Indians. He produced a black, silk scarf, stretching it taut. "I must blindfold you," he said. Shane turned her head and he bound the garment twice round her eyes and dark hair, pinning it with expert fingers.

From the sounds—and the smell—they turned back through the bazaar area; she felt them go over the Jumna Bridge and join a road on which thick traffic was moving and, after half an hour, turn on to a rutted road over which they travelled for several miles before halting. Someone opened the car door; a hand grasped Shane's and pulled her out of the car, up a flight of steps, along a smooth floor, down some dozen steps and along a passage where they had to walk in a single file. A door clicked open, someone gave her a shove and she stumbled inside.

Brodie caught her in his arms and kissed her before removing the blindfold. "Paul, I thought you were dead," she got out. Then she had to sit down on the one chair the basement room possessed, her legs feeling too weak to support her. Brodie sat down on the bed; he pointed a finger at his ear then at the central light, indicating it probably contained a listening device. "I'm glad you're here," he whispered. "In Delhi, they could have murdered you easily. Here, at least, we have a chance."

"Who are these people?"

"I don't know," he whispered. He explained how they had trapped him in the temple and as he tried to flee across the roof they had hit him over the head. All he had seen of the place was this basement. They treated him reasonably well; he had three meals a day, two bottles of beer, tea and coffee, and nobody had tried to interrogate him. He had seen the elegant native as well, and they had another couple of guards who looked a bit like Shigo. But where this was, he had no idea. He had looked out the two small basement windows, set high up and barred; but trees and shrubs obscured what view he might have had.

Brodie switched on the two electric fans, saying their noise would make it more difficult for them to eavesdrop on their conversation. Shane described what she had done after he had leapt from the tonga. When she found blood all over the temple, she really believed the dacoits had robbed then murdered him.

"No, they weren't dacoits," he said. "And they weren't this crowd, either. I think the first lot had just been given orders to kill us all."

"Kill us! Why?"

"Because we'd been too nosey for some people," he whispered.

"The epidemics?"

"That's what I think."

"But these people who have kidnapped you must want something as well," she said.

"That's what we're waiting to find out," he said. "I told them I wouldn't collaborate unless I had proof you had not been harmed. So, they brought you here." He looked at her, quizzically. "I hope you didn't mind."

"I was almost off my head thinking you were dead," she whispered. She rose and came over to kiss him. "What do we do now?" she whispered.

"Stall them as long as we can and wait until something breaks for us and we can escape."

Their conversation ended when the bolt slid back and an Indian entered wheeling a tray with mulligatawnay soup in a tureen and roast lamb on a platter under a burnished helmet. Brodie pointed at this then grinned at Shane. "I told you it's a good hotel. Round-the-clock waiter service." He thumbed at the two other men, clad like the waiter in ordinary tropical suits. "They're the maître d'hôtel and the wine waiter," he said. He ordered them beer and bottled water while the waiter set the table with a linen cloth and good cutlery.

"But they look like the staff of some residence," Shane whispered when the men had all departed.

"Probably a Russian one run by the KGB," he said. "But don't let it spoil your appetite."

"I'm beginning to agree with you, Paul—there's something very curious about those outbreaks."

He stopped her with a finger to his mouth then indented the word VIRUS on the tablecloth with a fork, signalling that she must not mention it. After the roast lamb and vegetables, they had fruit and coffee. Brodie looked at his watch. "In twenty minutes, at ten o'clock, they put out the main light," he said.

When they cleared away the coffee things, two men escorted them to a small shower-room and waited discreetly outside while they washed. Shane pushed together the two camp beds they had provided in the basement room. At ten, the central light went out leaving only a tiny, blue night bulb. They made love as softly as they could lest their room was "bugged" and people might be eavesdropping in other ways. "It reminds me of China," Shane whispered. Brodie replied that he agreed, but secretly he hoped it would not prove so dangerous.

On that occasion, the Maoist Chinese had taken them prisoner, forcing them to collaborate in making a vaccine they might have used to protect their population and use the lethal virus they had discovered as a biological weapon. Brodie had then manoeuvred them out of the situation by a series of brilliant moves; but they had been lucky to get away, and even then they had to force-march over some of the highest mountain passes in the world, from Sinkiang into Hunza. Whatever they faced now, he did not wish for another trek like that. "Better get some sleep," he said. "They keep hospital hours in this hotel. Breakfast comes up at six."

For two days they saw no-one but the waiters and guards who brought them meals and escorted them to the toilets and shower-room. However, after dinner on the second day, their door opened and the man who had kept the rendezvous with Shane appeared.

"Come with me," he ordered. They followed him along a narrow passage and up a flight of stairs that took them into an entrance hall with a marble staircase going up to a balcony and an upper floor. Crossing the hall, they made for a double door which gave access to a large room with French windows overlooking a terrace and stepped gardens. A man was standing gazing over these gardens beyond which lay the Jumna River plain and the high buildings, monuments and minarets of Delhi, backlighted by the setting sun. As he turned, even against the light, both Brodie and Shane gasped, recognizing the tall, patrician outline. And who, having heard it once, could ever have mistaken the drawling accent with which he said, "Nice to see you again, Paul, dear boy. And you, too, Dr Kingslake."

It was Cready-Smythe, his old secret-service boss.

X

SHANE TURNED ON her heel and would have marched from the room had not the elegant native who had escorted them barred her way. Twice she had encountered Cready-Smythe and on both occasions had disliked the man and his dubious profession; above all, she took exception to the way he had manoeuvred and manipulated Paul when he worked for the SIS, and even afterwards by enlisting him against his will. The Hon. Edwin Hubert Hilary Cready-Smythe's long aristocratic lineage impressed her just as little as his smarmy style and subtle double-talk; she wondered why Paul had ever fallen for them. She knew, too, that every time he crossed their path it meant trouble. "I might have guessed you were behind this kidnapping," she snapped.

"Kidnapping!" Cready-Smythe repeated, his rectangular face creasing into a smile. He screwed one of his special cigarettes (he had them hand made in Bond Street) into his ebony holder and lit it. "We saved Paul's life, or didn't he know it?" Turning to Brodie, he said, "You were towing three lots of agents behind you all the time you were in Delhi as though you were losing your touch, Paul."

"You mean four lots," Brodie countered, sarcastically.

"Nobody counts his own side, Paul."

"I've got no side."

"A pity, you're the best field agent I ever had," Cready-Smythe murmured, and even Shane thought that, for once, he meant what he said.

"Don't listen to his flattery," she burst out, then turned to Brodie. "Anyway, what do you both mean, four lots of people were following us?"

Brodie's eyes flicked towards the native who had conducted them from the basement, but he caught Cready-Smythe's head twitch signifying he could talk without restraint. "Well," he said, "Chebrakov knew what was going on—so we had the Russian Embassy's tame Indians watching us."

"Chebrakov knows only this much of the story," Cready-Smythe said, blinkering his blue eyes behind his hands. "But his bosses do and the USSR runs a big staff in Delhi with a lot of our old pals in it."

"You mean, the KGB?" Shane asked. The SIS man nodded assent.

"How strong are Dr Huang and the Chinese?"

"Strong enough to keep a watching brief, Paul."

"You mean, the Chinese were having us followed, too!" Shane gasped.

"By another lot of Indians," Cready-Smythe affirmed, then turned to Brodie. "And the third?" he asked.

"The real Indians," Brodie replied. "After all, they'd two outbreaks of this funny disease on their soil, and another just over the frontier."

"They didn't need to make a big operation of it."

"Well, they had Slattery with us most of the time, or listening in."

"Slattery!" Shane cried. "Is he a spy?"

"He does the Indian government small favours from time to time, and they leave him alone with his liquor bottles," Cready-Smythe drawled.

"How can you people ever trust anybody?" she exclaimed.

"We don't—do we, Paul?"

"How did you get to know about Shane and myself and what we'd found?" Brodie asked.

"Instinct, or intuition."

"So you had your man"—Brodie gestured at the stranger—"and his friends tail along to keep an eye on the others."

"We knew that if you both stumbled on anything vital to them, you'd be in danger," Cready-Smythe said. "And if we hadn't just happened to see your driver murdered and follow your tonga and run across you in that temple, those thugs would have murdered you, Paul. And then you, Dr Kingslake. And I doubt if anybody would ever have discovered your bodies."

"Is he trying to scare us, Paul?"

"No, what he says is about right."

"Then why doesn't somebody inform the police?" Shane said.

"For a good dozen reasons," Cready-Smythe replied. "For one, those men were paid to murder Brodie and you, and Slattery if necessary. But even they don't know who their paymasters are. And the police would never discover who the dacoits really were or who hired them. Secondly, we don't want the men behind those killers to learn that we know what we do, and some clumsy Indian policeman might alert them, or one of his colleagues might do it for a small consideration. Thirdly, they don't know where you are, or even if you're in the land of the living, so we can't urge you to go and allege attempted murder. Fourthly, the police might ask several awkward questions about who killed the Indian in that temple . . ."

"One of your hired men," Shane said, mordantly.

"Self-defence, m'dear. Self-defence." Cready-Smythe flicked his spent cigarette through the window on to the verandah. "I couldn't stand by and see my old friend, Paul, tortured and murdered, now could I?"

To that, Shane had no answer. After all, they had saved Paul's life. "But don't start boasting you did it out of loyalty," she said. "You did it because you want something from him."

"Nothing Paul isn't prepared to give of his own volition."

"Why him?"

"Because you and he have half-solved the problem of those funny epidemics already—which is why you'd both be risking your lives if you walked out of here without an armed escort."

"We'll leave the other half to you," Shane said. "Neither myself nor Paul is going to get involved in any of the little war games you're so fond of playing."

"Too late, you're both involved already," Cready-Smythe said, blandly. "You might as well have written your death warrant as give WHO those two dangerous bits of information about the virus you discovered in that northern valley, and about the birds." Cready-Smythe strolled across the marble floor to a table with a cardboard carton on it. Ripping this open, he extracted several books. Four of them he handed to Brodie and two to Shane. "I thought you, Paul, should have some up-to-date bird books—those second-hand ones you acquired in Jaipur weren't much good."

"What are these for?" Shane asked, pointing to her two books.

"The latest thing on adenoviruses and something called molecular biology that I'll never even begin to understand."

"I don't see the connection," Shane said.

Brodie looked at Cready-Smythe for enlightenment, but that equine face and those blue eyes betrayed no hint of what was happening in his cryptic mind. After ten years of collaboration with Cready-Smythe, you realized every utterance required untangling and deciphering. Never once in Brodie's experience had he told the whole truth and hardly ever had he fashioned a straightforward statement without a hook in it somewhere. This man, apart from his Oxford Double First in languages and history and his patrician background, had perhaps the best brain in Her Majesty's Secret Intelligence Service, and was moreover clever enough to disguise it. Brodie could roughly guess where his old boss was heading, and he realized he had not travelled eight thousand miles to the centre of India in the drugging heat unless he thought it vital. That could only mean a security threat, and probably an international one. From the moment Brodie had spotted Dettwiler, his four men and their sentinels, he suspected something other than a simple virus, accidentally spread, had provoked the Runghar outbreak; his chance sighting of Krahl at Cochin and the appearance of someone like Chebrakov at Riswana confirmed this hunch. However, at the moment, something intrigued him just as much: how would the suave and devious Cready-Smythe lure Shane into his net along with himself? Brodie made no move, no comment but merely watched the duel develop.

"What have adenoviruses and molecular biology to do with shingles outbreaks?" Shane persisted.

"What wouldn't we give to answer that question ourselves?"

Cready-Smythe murmured. "And especially how birds can be contaminated with such viruses and spread them as though they were guided missiles."

"What are you implying—that someone is deliberately infecting birds with adenoviruses and shingles?"

"It is possible—isn't it?"

That set Shane reflecting. She glanced at Brodie who merely shrugged his ignorance, then at Cready-Smythe. He was now sitting behind the large desk doodling on a pad with a felt pen; he was drawing something like seagulls dropping guano on the heads of several matchstick figures, some of whom were standing while others had dropped and presumably died.

"No, I don't think it is, and anyway if it were, I wouldn't believe it."

"It does sound rather diabolical, Dr Kingslake."

Shane's eyes had gone pensive and she was wrinkling her forehead in perplexity. "But even if they did manage to infect the birds, how could they control where they went, how they bred and all that. They might lay eggs which people would eat." She shook her head. "No, it's crazy."

"I'm no ornithologist." Cready-Smythe went on doodling, depicting several other types of bird, including pigeons and swallows. "But birds have well-known migration routes, I believe."

"They also return to the country and even the district where they breed," Shane objected. "And they'd therefore carry the virus back with them."

"That is a problem," Cready-Smythe conceded. "So, I presume any country using the birds as contaminating agent would have to vaccinate against the infecting virus."

"They would—but so far as I know nobody has vaccinated a whole population against chicken-pox or shingles, the two illnesses we've found here."

"We wondered, too, how they'd manage to avoid epidemics," Cready-Smythe said. "They must have some system."

Brodie could observe that, despite her aversion to the SIS man and his profession, Shane was becoming as fascinated by the problem as he was himself. Cready-Smythe was capitalizing on the fact that medical research workers—micro-biologists, virologists, epidemiologists—all played detective roles by collecting nature's secrets and piecing them together to find the answers to various diseases. Now he had her pondering what he had chosen to divulge. Yet she still shook her head. "I still can't and don't believe it," she said, finally.

"I would give anything to agree with you," Cready-Smythe murmured. "We'd all like to think your lecture and your paper hadn't caused that flurry in the World Health Organization and somebody didn't hire that bunch of thugs to make sure you and Paul didn't reveal any more secrets." He nodded to the handsome native who had stood silent and immobile throughout the conversation. Now, he came forward to hand Cready-Smythe a photograph from the folder he carried. When passed to Shane, she gazed at what appeared a blown-up identity picture of a young Indian. "You've seen him before," said Cready-Smythe. "Dead—on the stairs of the Lok district temple."

"Why couldn't the police identify him when you've managed to do so?" she queried.

"The simple answer is they didn't want to for political reasons. But he's well-known. His name's Nair Trimurthi and he's a militant communist from Trivandrum near the tip of India. Among other things, he's a friend of your erstwhile escort, Dr Krishnan. If you want any more proof . . ."

"Which communists were these thugs supposed to be working for—the Chinese or the Russians?"

Cready-Smythe looked at her with his most disarming grin. "Unfortunately we didn't have time to ask him that before he passed on—and I doubt very much if he could have told us."

Shane threw the photo back across the desk to him, angrily. "Are we free to go?" she asked.

"But you always have been," Cready-Smythe replied in a wounded tone. "My friend here only brought you to this house in . . . well, let's say protective custody." He pointed to the picture on his desk. "But his friends will still be looking for both of you to fulfil their contract to murder you—especially if they find out you've seen us."

Shane turned, appealingly, to Brodie. "Paul, I want to get back to Hunza and forget about all this," she said. "At least we'll be safe there."

"I wouldn't be too sure," Cready-Smythe murmured. Rising, he walked to the terrace window. Darkness was settling slowly on the plain and the lights of Delhi made a red bruise in the sky. "Anyway, you can't go tonight, and there's no Sunday flight to Pindi or over the hump to Gilgit." He turned and smiled at them. "We'll allot you a better room so why not put your feet up here for two or three days and we can all go up together to . . . what do you call it? . . . Shangri-la."

"What are you going up there for?" Shane said, suddenly apprehensive.

"Didn't I tell you?—the mir has asked me to be his guest for a few days, and I thought I might just go for a short amble in the Karakorams—or the Kun Lun Mountains, or the Pamirs," Cready-Smythe said, flashing a grin at Brodie. "Anyway, I think you should wait for something I'm expecting in the post—something you might like to have a look at, since you've covered so much ground looking for the answer to those weird epidemics."

"What's that?" Shane asked, eagerly and spontaneously, and Brodie realized his old spymaster had her hooked and almost ready for the gaff.

"One of the infected birds we captured," Cready-Smythe murmured. And on that suspenseful note he bade them both goodnight and left them in the hands of his strange native friend.

XI

FOR FOUR DAYS no-one bothered them; they had transferred to a large bedroom with a huge bathroom overlooking the gardens at the front of the villa; on the south side of the house, surrounded by locust trees, bean trees and ornamental shrubs lay a swimming pool which they used in the mornings and late afternoons. One of the native servants had recovered their luggage from the Nataraj Hotel and brought them whatever they wanted from Delhi, presumably paying with SIS funds. With the exception of the living-room, which Cready-Smythe used as a study, and his room near theirs on the first floor, they had the run of the house. From its architecture, its marble and mosaic work and its opulent furnishings, Brodie guessed it belonged to some wealthy Indian or foreign merchant and had been rented for a few months by the High Commissioner's office at the behest of London.

Although no-one appeared to be keeping surveillance on them their bedroom door was locked at ten o'clock and only opened when a servant appeared with their breakfast at seven. If they strolled down to the iron railings surrounding the grounds, they inevitably encountered one of the coloured servants; at night, Brodie had spotted men with dogs patrolling the perimeter fence. Brodie puzzled about the staff. They spoke Urdu among themselves, but like a second language. They were not Hindus, for they smoked cigarettes normally and did not "drink" the tobacco through their clenched fist like caste Hindus. Cready-Smythe never did anything uncalculated, so if he had brought in foreigners, it signified he did not trust Indians, but what else? What was Cready-Smythe's game? That cryptic remark about going for a stroll through three of the most formidable mountain ranges in the world implied he intended to penetrate either Russia or China. To do that, he must have had a smell of something really serious.

They had access to a library of several thousand novels and non-fiction books, but Brodie noticed that even in their hours of relaxation, Shane immersed herself in the thick text-books on virology and molecular biology Cready-Smythe had ferried out from London. As for himself, he was ploughing through the bird books, trying to trace the sort of seabird Asari had described and working through the species that migrated over long distances; he concentrated on the routes from Arctic Russia, Siberia and Mongolia across Asiatic Russia and China then down through India.

"The only thing I think it could be is some form of tern," he muttered to her, lifting his head from one of the bird books. "I mean, the birds Asari saw."

"They keep to the coasts, don't they?" she objected. "They're called sea-swallows."

"Some of them fish the way the old boy said, and some of them even croak like him."

"Maybe, but from what I know, they never fly south until autumn at the earliest," she said.

They read each other's books and swopped and compared notes on the sort of birds that might carry diseases as well as certain new viruses that might just fit the type they had discovered through their primitive lab tests in Hunza. Quite often, Shane initiated these discussions and Brodie found her even more intrigued than he with what they had heard from Cready-Smythe about the epidemics. "But he's holding something back, Paul," she insisted. "What do you think it is?"

Brodie could not answer her. Conforming to the rules of the game, his old spymaster would only reveal what he thought necessary to ensure their co-operation, and nothing more. Brodie did know, however, that Cready-Smythe's presence here meant the assignment had the highest priority, controlled by the SIS supreme chief, C, and under British Cabinet orders. One incident suggested they must have given Cready-Smythe a completely free hand. On their third night, an hour or two after they had gone to sleep, a car woke Brodie. From the window, he watched it come slowly up the drive to stop outside the front door. Two figures emerged, escorting a third into the building. Brodie heard the living-room door click shut behind them. He stepped on to the balcony which overhung the terrace; he could swing over and drop the five or six feet, but how to get back? He was deliberating whether to put together a makeshift rope or wake Shane and enlist her assistance when a shaft of light fell across the front doorstep. Out came the two men conducting the third. He was wearing a blindfold, but even this did not hide the face of a Chinese or a Japanese. Brodie watched the car disappear, thinking Cready-Smythe was keeping some very strange company. A bunch of imported natives and now a Japanese or Chinese who was brought out here, blindfold, for a ten-minute meeting.

On their fourth afternoon a package arrived by car for Cready-Smythe. Brodie and Shane were lying under parasols by the swimming pool when they heard his summons to the living-room. He was bending over his desk, unwrapping layers of straw then cotton-wool from an object in a plywood box. His head lifted and he grinned at them. "Amazing what one does find in the diplomatic bag these days, isn't it?" Plunging a hand into the box, he pulled out a dead bird between ten and twelve inches long. It had a white, downy breast and a mottled, brown back; its beak was long, straight and sharp and its long, spindly legs were a tan colour. "Well, you're our birdman, Paul. What is it?"

Brodie peered at it. "It's a wading bird—looks like a redshank." He was disappointed that it looked nothing like the birds Asari had seen at Riswana; he had expected some sort of seabird, a gull or tern, much bigger than the one Cready-Smythe was holding. Asari must have got it wrong.

"No, it's not a redshank or a greenshank," Cready-Smythe said, pulling out the bird's stiff legs to show they were neither the reddish-orange of the first bird or the greenish hue of the second. "Have another go."

"Where was it caught?"

"In the marshes of a lake near Bulawayo in southern Zimbabwe—six, seven weeks ago."

"Then I don't have a clue what it is," Brodie said, after reflection.

"It's *philomachus pugnax*, a very promiscuous and pugnacious species—in other words, a ruff."

"It can't be," Brodie protested. "Ruffs shouldn't be anywhere near the southern hemisphere at this time of the year. They only go to Africa and India to winter."

"Where should they be in summer?"

"Siberia—anyway, somewhere up in the tundra. From what I've read, they migrate south and south-west across China and Russia into India and Africa." Taking the bird from Cready-Smythe, he examined it from every angle. A long, surgical incision from under the breastbone to the tail halted his eye, but he assumed the ornithologist who had performed the post-mortem—or perhaps a taxidermist—had made this. "I just don't begin to understand," he said. "It's too big for the female of the species—the reeve—and if it's the male, it should have its summer plumage."

"Of course," Shane put in. "They have a big, red ruff round their necks in the breeding season."

"Red, brown, black and other colours," Brodie corrected. "It also has rear-tufts and this bird has nothing like that. Another thing, they like to fly and mate in company."

While they had been discussing the bird, Cready-Smythe was casting his eye over the two typescript sheets that had accompanied the dead bird. "Our tame ornithologists in London agree with everything you say—but it's still a ruff, that is, a male. They also state that it has had its reproductive organs removed surgically." He paused and pinched the flesh of his long chin between thumb and forefinger. "Now, why would anyone want to castrate this poor bird?" he mused.

"To stop him from breeding," Brodie said.

"And spreading a virus around if he had it in his system?" the SIS chief suggested.

"Unlikely," Shane said. "Birds normally contaminate each other, and people, by contact."

"But not always," Brodie put in.

"I suppose not," she conceded. "Viruses can be transmitted through the hereditary process from parent to offspring."

"Viruses like the adeno . . ." Cready-Smythe was groping for the term.

"Adenoviruses," Shane said. "I don't see why not. What makes you ask that?"

"Because this bird was carrying one or several adenoviruses."

"How can you prove that?" Brodie asked.

"Simply because a good dozen people around where it landed got headcolds and a thing called Pink-eye that I've never even heard of."

"But they could have picked that up from anything or anybody," Brodie objected.

"They tell me it's very rare in that part of southern Africa," Cready-Smythe said. "Anyway, there's better proof. The white farmer's little daughter who found this bird sick by the lakeside, brought it home—and she, her father, mother, brother and their servants all developed Pink-eye. Too long a coincidence, isn't it?"

"I've never heard of a bird carrying an adenovirus like the Pink-eye type," Shane said.

"Is it serious?"

She shook her head. "No, it's a virulent form of conjunctivitis," she replied. "But it's produced by the adenovirus that causes colds and fevers and sometimes lung infection."

Brodie was still holding the bird, about the size of a pigeon; he extended its long legs and saw that someone had ringed it. Not with the normal alloy band round its leg, but a red plastic ring stamped with just the number 7 instead of the usual serial number. No indication of the organization that had done the ringing, or an address to contact if the bird were caught. Whoever wanted to keep track of this errant bird evidently did not want anyone else to discover where he came from. He saw Cready-Smythe's eye on him. "Any other Pink-eye outbreaks?" he asked.

"Funny you should ask that, Paul. In fact there are a couple of epidemics we know of, and probably others that nobody has bothered to report." Crossing the room to the globe map on a stand, he placed a finger on the straits between Africa and Arabia at the bottom of the Red Sea. In Jibuti, several French Foreign legionnaires had gone down with head colds, and a couple with Pink-eye. Their medical officer had made a report which came to the notice of one of Cready-Smythe's men who passed it to London. Then Brazzaville, the WHO regional office for Africa, received a report about a small outbreak of Pink-eye and summer colds from the Tanzanian side of Lake Victoria, as well as hearing about the Zimbabwe outbreak.

"Have you got a small-scale world map?" Brodie asked. Cready-Smythe went to open his writing bureau and produce a folding map, which Brodie spread on the table. Watched by the SIS man and Shane, he plotted the three Indian outbreaks then the three African ones; he drew lines connecting the six points, projecting them north until the two main lines intersected in the Soviet Union at a point about a hundred miles west of Omsk in the middle of the Siberian steppe. Cready-Smythe smiled, but shook his head.

"Unfortunately, birds don't always fly in straight lines, Paul," he murmured. "Take ruffs, for instance. They don't like crossing long stretches of water like the Mediterranean. And in any case, there may be more than just one bird—there may be dozens, and several different species."

"Well, where do you think the birds that caused the African and Indian outbreaks came from?" Shane asked.

"We're still working on that one."

"If your theory's right and the birds have been contaminated purposely, then it must be near a border," Brodie said.

Cready-Smythe looked at him, quizzically. "What makes you say that, Paul?"

"Because migrating birds often fly in short hops and no-one would want them to infect people in their country of origin."

"I think the whole story's crazy," Shane exclaimed. "I don't see how anybody can hope to control the flight of migrating birds, let alone infect them."

"To answer those questions you'd have to go to an ornithologist, or a molecular biologist—like yourself, Dr Kingslake," Cready-Smythe said. He took the dead ruff and packed it into the plywood box then folded and packeted the typescript and thanked them before disappearing upstairs into his own room.

Shane gazed after the long, slim figure. "That man makes me want to hit him, the way he plays his little game of secrets," she said. "Does he have to encode everything he says?"

"The trick is never to ask straight questions," Brodie grinned. "That way, you sometimes get the right answers."

But Shane was justified in her anger. With his SIS mentality and his personal penchant for arcane games, Cready-Smythe could not help talking in conundrums and often gave the impression they were on the other side. Some of his own agents felt they had two enemies: Cready-Smythe and the opposition. Yet, paradoxically, for Brodie it became a challenge to play Cready-Smythe at his own game and fit the pieces of the puzzle together before he did. Despite the man's patrician style and the fact that he never let his own right hand know what his left hand was doing, there was a bond between him and Brodie, the sort of relationship that a psychiatrist and his patient often develop. He could see why Shane might resent that, too.

When they joined Cready-Smythe for dinner that evening, he produced a bottle of pure-malt Scotch and poured it generously before they sat down to eat. To their astonishment, from somewhere he had procured Scotch smoked salmon and a splendid Montrachet; they looked at each other when the waiter unveiled a dozen quail on a platter and uncorked two bottles of fine claret; they finished with a cheeseboard of English cheese, then a sorbet.

"More game and other surprises from the diplomatic bag," Shane said, sarcastically. "What are we celebrating?"

"Ah! didn't I tell you?" Cready-Smythe drawled.

"No, you didn't," Brodie interjected. "But we guessed it was the last supper, and we've already packed our things." He was gratified to see that Cready-Smythe looked suitably crestfallen.

XII

AT TIMES, CREADY-SMYTHE gave the impression he would never survive the first stage of their journey into the remote Hunza Valley. Twice before he had made the trip in the rickety Dakota over the last Himalayan humps from Rawalpindi to Gilgit, and each time with his eyes tightly shut. But now a mist obliterated the Babusar Pass, their greatest hazard, and as they climbed into it blind, Brodie could see his former chief's face turn as green as the Indus below them. It shook him visibly when they surfaced from the mist into a blue sky and found the jagged ridges of Nanga Parbat at their wingtip and miles above their flight line. Downdraughts from its snows and glaciers set them wobbling over the pass and Cready-Smythe groping rearwards, vomit bag in hand. At Gilgit airstrip, Shigo was waiting for them with two jeeps; he had opened the mir's resthouse where they would stay the night before tackling the mountains and gorges the following day. "Why don't you get the Pakistani governor to give you a chopper and do the trip up the valley in comfort?" Brodie suggested.

"No, this one I must do the hard way, Paul."

"You know we start three hours before dawn," Brodie said and the other man listened, incredulously, as he explained they might run into avalanches and have to ford fresh torrents if they waited for the sun to melt the snow and glaciers over their route and slacken the piles of loose scree.

In the small hours, their two jeeps took them from Gilgit to where the switchback road ended at Chalt oasis. From there, they had to strap all their gear on mules and start their trek through the Hunza gorges, over goat-tracks in the hills and along narrow ledges overhanging the foaming river. By early afternoon, Cready-Smythe could march no longer; in the rarefied air ten thousand feet up, his breath was coming in short spurts and he was hobbling. They had to distribute their gear between the two lead mules and rig a makeshift saddle for him on the third animal. At Hini oasis, Shigo found them an empty house; he bathed Cready-Smythe's blistered feet and fed him supper in his sleeping-bag.

However, the next day, he kept going without complaint and even Shane had to admit his courage. When they broke out of Murtazabad gorge and had their first sight of the largest oasis in the Hunza Valley, they rested for quarter of an hour. Cready-Smythe gazed at the long, sun-filled valley with its stepped fields where Himalayan flowers made an aura of red, blue and pink against the green of the fields and the orchards of apricot, peach, and pear trees. Massive, snow-bound peaks etched against a blue sky, set off this vast garden. "All right, it does look like Xanadu or Shangri-la," Cready-Smythe murmured. "I've got to give you that."

That evening, they reached Karimabad, the Hunza capital. Cready-Smythe had not lied; the mir had allotted him his guest-house during his stay; he waved this aside, declaring he did not want to make himself a nuisance and therefore preferred to lodge with his good friends, Paul Brodie and Dr Kingslake. "Friends indeed," Shane spat as she heard him enlist Shigo's help to install his gear in one of their best rooms in the disused Baltit palace. It seemed they could not get rid of the man. Worse still, he soon suborned Shigo who could not do enough for him. When Shane complained, gently, their Hunza orderly grinned and said, "Smythe is burra sahib—great man—like Paul."

Brodie watched the cat-and-mouse game between both of them without uttering. Cready-Smythe was working to some overall strategy, though he gave nothing away. He had Shigo and Wali, the wazir's head of household, transport mountaineering equipment from Mankad's stores in Gilgit, not only for himself but for half a dozen people. And, as soon as it arrived, he began to use it for two and three and four-day trips into the mountains north and east of the main Hunza Valley. Brodie envied both him and Shigo as they set off to do a spot of botanizing or bird-watching in Cready-

Smythe's joking language. "What do we do if we meet the Abominable Snowman?" he asked.

"Keep quiet about it," Brodie replied. "We don't want the one lost valley in the world full of tourists."

From Shigo, he learned that Smythe-sahib had ventured as far as the Mintaka Pass, the crossroads on the old Silk Trail between China, Russia, Afghanistan and Pakistan; it seemed he had good enough maps to explore parts of the Hunza territory that not even Shigo knew. He also had friends in those places.

"What sort of friends?" Brodie asked.

"Is looking one like Pathan or Afridi man from Afghanistan. One other like Turki from Sinkiang way."

Although itching to discover what his old spymaster was doing and to play some part in solving the mystery of the birds and those outbreaks of illness, he nevertheless realized that he would be kept guessing until, despite himself, he was poking his nose then his head into one of the SIS man's finely-spun webs. Since their return to the valley, a helicopter had made the trip from Gilgit to Baltit bringing supplies and mail. After their mail deliveries, Cready-Smythe spent hours obviously decoding various messages, though he said never a word of this to Brodie or Shane.

They noticed that even his two weeks in the valley had wrought changes in his long-boned figure; those trips with Shigo had toughened his body and lengthened his wind and bronzed his face, chest and arms; several times he even gave the wazir a run for it coming up the steep slope to Baltit. Brodie could sense he was preparing for some long and arduous trip, especially when he cut his smoking and only allowed himself the occasional cigarette after a meal.

"It's all these apricots, Paul," he joked one evening at dinner when Brodie commented on his fitness. He, who had always scoffed at those who imputed Hunza longevity and health to the dried apricots they ate by the ton. "I must plant a couple of trees in my London garden."

"What's the idea—do you want to be first up Godwin Austen?" Brodie asked, drily.

"Funny you should ask that. The mountain I'd like to have a go at is Mustagh Ata."

"What! That ice mountain on the Chinese border with Russia," Shane exclaimed, glancing with astonishment at Brodie, failing once again to catch the overtones of Cready-Smythe's utterances. Brodie knew that the cryptic, tongue-in-cheek remark meant the SIS man had some inkling of where those birds had started their bizarre and unseasonal migration.

"It's worse than that mountain over there," Shane went on, pointing to Rakaposhi, the immense pyramid which reached into the high clouds flaming in the lengthening sun which also struck light from the great glaciers sheathing its face. "Mustagh Ata has killed half a dozen real mountaineers," Shane exclaimed, then paused, struck by a thought. "You're not taking Shigo on a mad stunt like that."

"If he asks to go, how can I refuse?"

"You'd have to get Chinese permission," Brodie put in.

"Good point. I'm actually waiting for it." He chose two apricots from the succulent pile on the table and chewed them, meditatively. "I was thinking they might even be persuaded to lend me half a dozen porters and one of their climbers for the job."

"You probably realize that if you take a couple of steps to your left, you could land in Russia."

"I suppose we could, if we happened to lose our way and blunder across the frontier."

"And just happen to stumble on a certain type of aviary," Brodie remarked with heavy sarcasm; from Shane's face, he deduced she had finally grasped the import of Cready-Smythe's convoluted statements.

"But you would never get into and out of Russia alive with a phony manoeuvre like that," she gasped.

"Paul did it."

"I'm a field man who thinks on his feet, and you're a desk wallah who wouldn't know a bacterium from a bird-dropping even if you managed to get near enough," Brodie said.

"You *were* a field man, Paul darling," Shane corrected.

"Paul is still one of us in spirit," Cready-Smythe retorted. "If he weren't, I wouldn't be opening my heart like this."

At this, Shane could not contain herself and burst out laughing. "Opening what?" she spluttered.

Cready-Smythe looked genuinely wounded, turning to appeal to Brodie. "You understand, don't you, Paul?" he said. "If you were coming with me I could tell you everything—but how could I take the responsibility of anything happening to you now you're off the payroll?"

"He's twisting your arm, darling," Shane warned.

"He did save our lives in Delhi."

"We don't owe each other a thing," Cready-Smythe murmured. "However, I want to prove I still trust you."

"Trust him!" Shane cried. "There's one phone out of this valley, and nobody can move without at least fifteen thousand people up and down Hunza knowing about it. Who could we tell?"

"A shared secret is a contradiction in terms," Cready-Smythe said in an undertone. Excusing himself, he disappeared into the house to return carrying a box which he opened with a key. Brodie saw him quickly flip over a file on the top of the box; but not before he had seen the top-secret code sign and the two words: PROJECT ICARUS. Brodie lit a kerosene pressure lamp while the other man rummaged in the box to extract several maps of the region and a few blown-up photographs which bore numbers corresponding with the maps. Before spreading all this on the table, the SIS man went to the door giving on to the terrace and closed it ignoring the fact that, like most doors in Hunza, it had no lock and its bolt did not work. He came back to deploy the maps and pictures across the fruit-wood table, co-ordinating both so that they could compare them. Cready-Smythe explained London had fed migration data from ruffs through a computer, also programming it with the locations of the three African and three Indian outbreaks. This had given them a rough-and-ready idea of where the birds had started their flight and with this information they had asked the Americans to run satellite scans of a Soviet area about fifty miles north of the

Afghan border with Russia and thirty to forty miles west of the Chinese border. In these satellite pictures, taken from an orbit two hundred miles high, they had finally hit something resembling what they were seeking.

Cready-Smythe laid a finger on two dark patches on the photographs, two small lakes, one shoe-shaped, the other like a spoon lying in a broad, ice-age valley amid high mountains. "Istky and Oksay Kul lakes," he said. Brodie peered at the pictures through a magnifying-glass and Shane also bent over them, fascinated. Round the indentation, like an arch, in the shoe-shaped lake, they could discern buildings in a group south of one of the streams feeding the lake.

"Three of those look as if they had domed roofs," Brodie said, pointing to buildings in the centre of the camp.

"Glass cupolas," Cready-Smythe specified. "We think they're aviaries." His fingernail tracked over the lake in a half-circle. "They've rigged a sort of boom across the lake—like those shark-protection nets around bathing-spots."

Brodie ran his magnifying-glass over the whole of the camp beside the lake, then studied individual buildings within the compound; he made out several wooden structures, among them a long building he took for a barrack-room. A track ran alongside the lake above the compound and disappeared along the deep valley, presumably linking the place with the Oksu Valley road which ran north into the steppe and south to Afghanistan. "No power lines," Brodie muttered. "They'll use a diesel generator."

Cready-Smythe indicated the two lookout posts on the mountain tops either side of the valley. "They obviously don't want Tajik farmers or Kirghiz shepherds, or anybody else wandering into that area unannounced," he murmured. From his box, he had produced another series of pictures, this time infra-red. These showed the heat patches produced by trucks, the generator building and the various heated buildings in the camp. Beside the generator building in the middle of the camp, they identified a huge tank, obviously for storing diesel fuel. Brodie noted that the three buildings with glass cupolas gave a high heat-rating on the infra-red photos; on one or two of the pictures taken at night with ordinary cameras, they shone like searchlights. Just beyond them, two low buildings looked like labs.

"That looks like a chopper," Brodie said, pointing to the long tapering shape of a helicopter on a patch of level ground inside the camp. "I suppose they have to bring their material, their provisions and mail in that way since there are only tracks over those mountains and they must be difficult going for months in the year."

"It's wild country," Cready-Smythe said, producing maps of that part of the roof of the world. Only the river valleys lay below twelve thousand feet; many of the mountains rose to more than twenty thousand feet. A single good road ran through the region, south from the Karakul Lake along the Oksu Valley parallel with the Chinese frontier about twenty miles inside Russia. Running the powerful lens over what lay between the camp and where they stood now, Brodie could well comprehend Cready-Smythe's sudden passion for mountaineering. "It's a bit of an assault-course there and back," he commented.

"If we have to walk."

"What other way is there?" Brodie asked. "You couldn't drive a tank over those peaks. If you're dropped by parachute they'll pick you up in five minutes; if you use a chopper, they'll blow you out of the sky before you've crossed the border."

"And if you ever get there, you'll probably find it's just a wild-life sanctuary run by bird conservationists," Shane remarked.

"In that case, I wonder what Nikolai Grigorevich Burov has been doing there for more than a year," Cready-Smythe said.

"Burov, the microbiologist?" Shane queried, and he nodded. "If it's the same, he worked as a postgraduate student with my late husband at Cambridge."

"It is the same, and now he's working there." He stabbed a finger at the camp, then turned to Brodie. "He disappeared from his Leningrad lab a couple of years ago, and we wondered where he'd got to. Then one of our men spotted him in Samarkand heading for Dushanbe, seventy miles from the camp." He glanced at Shane. "I wouldn't say for a moment that he's given up bugs for birds, would you?"

"He was very brilliant, they say."

"He must be—they gave him a Lenin Prize last year."

"Then what is he doing in that backwater?" Shane asked.

"Ah! If only we knew."

Shane rose to clear the table, then went to help Shigo with the washing-up, leaving the two men sitting just outside the circle of yellow light. After a few minutes, Cready-Smythe broke the silence. "When you were given an assignment, did you ever feel you were doing your last run?"

"Every time," Brodie replied. "But then it didn't bother me."

Cready-Smythe knew what he meant. Now Paul Brodie had put his life together again with Shane Kingslake, he had something to lose. When they had worked together, he hadn't much time for life or whether his own continued or stopped. Yet, ironically, it was the service for which he was risking his life that had resuscitated him. Cready-Smythe's mind flashed back to thirteen years before when he had answered a summons from one of their talent scouts in Glasgow; he had arrived there to discover Brodie in a prison hospital, wrapped in bandages, broken in spirit and facing half a dozen charges which would have carried several years in jail. From friends, the spymaster had pieced together his story; a brilliant medical student with a year to go before qualifying, he had just got engaged and was celebrating this and his academic success; he had even hired a car to take his future bride to the end-of-term dance at the Royal Infirmary. At the dance, somebody had decided to take the brilliant Brodie down a peg by spiking his drink with pure alcohol. And the car had finished up, wrecked, a mile or two outside Glasgow; his girl was dead when they reached the Royal Infirmary where she had worked as a nurse. Brodie had survived, cut out of the car, dead-drunk, his face burned and one leg badly smashed, wondering at first what had happened and later why he hadn't died. A self-punishing type, he would gladly have done his time in prison then committed slow suicide on the bottle or some other poison. It had taken hours and every bit of Cready-Smythe's persuasive talent to talk him into starting a new career—in Her Majesty's most secret intelligence service. And Brodie, with his flair for languages and his technical mind, had become, as Cready-Smythe confessed, the best field agent he had ever handled.

"I shanghaied you," Cready-Smythe muttered, then bit his tongue for the remark and the involuntary way it had escaped his mental censorship.

"You saved my life then, too," said Brodie, revealing that he, too, had been going over those thirteen years. Prague in '68, the Bangla-Desh War, the coup against Salvador Allende in Chile, the twilit world of Berlin before and after The Wall, Cyprus, Athens and the downfall of the Colonels—these and a score more assignments they had done together though they could never talk about them, even now. Cready-Smythe had landed him in some tight situations, often leaving him to extricate himself when he had to choose between his agent and delivering vital information. Nevertheless, they trusted each other and they both knew that neither could allow the other to walk over those mountains on his own.

"You can't go in there without a backstop and without taking out a life insurance policy," Brodie mused, almost to himself.

"I've got to go in, and I'm fully paid up."

"I meant the kind of insurance the Russians accept as valid."

"They only accept eye-for-eye and knock-for-knock insurance."

"That's what I meant." He rolled himself a cigarette, refusing his companion's offer of his Bond Street special brand. "How much money has C allotted you for this job?"

"As much as it takes—and full diplomatic backing."

"Does that include them down there?" Brodie pointed to the lights of the mir's palace and the wazir's residence and Cready-Smythe nodded. "Have you enough cash to pay for half a dozen sheep, fifty gallons of sherbet and a few bottles of Scotch?"

"Of course—but why?"

"Because I think you ought to reciprocate all the hospitality you've received in the valley and throw a party for a couple of hundred people," Brodie said, and would not elaborate. When he had finished his cigarette and was rising to go, he said, casually, over his shoulder, "By the way, have you had chicken-pox?"

For a moment Cready-Smythe hesitated, then replied, "Come to think, I don't remember ever having caught that. But why?"

"Nothing." Brodie nodded and bade the other man good-night, leaving him with a puzzled look on his face. Two Whys in one night from Cready-Smythe. That must make some sort of record.

XIII

IT HAD ALWAYS seemed a mystery to Brodie how news travelled like a powder train along the hundred kilometres from Chalt to the Chinese frontier in a valley with only one telephone line. Everyone seemed to have got wind of Smythe-sahib's birthday feast, for they came trekking through the gorges in dozens, mainly the headmen and village councillors who had received word-of-mouth invitations. For a whole day, the Baltit palace had sat in the aura of roasting sheep; Shigo, Wali and a small army of Hunza helpers had worked to deck out the terrace with tables laden with various cold meats, spiced vegetables, fruits, cakes and gallons of soft drinks, since Moslems mostly abstained from liquor. Cready-Smythe had more than done his bit, ordering the sheep and other meat rarely seen in the valley, and dipping into SIS funds to provide prizes at the children's gala and other events. He personally presented the polo prize after the game (invented in these valleys) which Hunza lost to Gilgit's crack team. An hour before the sun went off Rakaposhi, Shigo and Wali bore the first sheep on to the terrace. At Brodie's instigation, they solemnly presented Cready-Smythe with the first eye in front of the assembled guests; he made a pretence of swallowing it, but successfully palmed it into his pocket. "A dirty trick," he said to Brodie through his teeth.

"No dirtier than the time in Prague during the Soviet invasion when you planted two films showing Russian armoured vehicles in my kit and let me walk, innocently, through two police and customs points with them."

Cready-Smythe still did not know what Brodie had in mind; during the dismemberment and ingestion of several sheep, he watched him circulate and converse with Bahadur Ali and several other people. After sunset, when they lit the terrace lamps, Brodie motioned him into the house and through to the clinic and laboratories. To his surprise, he saw the wazir and two other men whom Brodie introduced as Ikhbal Khan, headman of Sherkut village, near Runghar where they had witnessed the first outbreak, and Yakub Sher, headman of Kandit, the neighbouring village. Sherkut had sixty-three villagers and Kandit forty-eight. With the headman at Brodie's invitation had come eight of their young villagers.

Brodie opened their freezer and extracted a test-tube in which a pink-tinged liquid had frozen solid, and two eggs on which he had marked "Runghar" and the date in blue pencil. Holding up the test-tube and an egg, he addressed the two headmen and the wazir. "This vessel and the two eggs contain the germs I took from the sick people at Runghar." There, he had to digress and explain to Yakub Sher's satisfaction how he had cultured the germs, which stretched his Hindustani somewhat. "Now, if I break this egg," he went on, "or open this test-tube and let its contents thaw and spread the germs in air or water, those people who have no immunity to the sickness will suffer from it. Only those protected will not suffer."

"How do we gain this protection?" Ikhbal Khan asked.

"Only by being injected with medicine, or by catching a mild form of the disease," Brodie replied. "Now the villagers of Runghar are safe and I would like Sherkut and Kandit to be as safe, too, by giving them the sickness." He apologized for not having enough medicine to inject the villagers, except the headman and the eight men who had come to the feast. He quizzed both headmen about the elderly people in their village, numbering twenty-two in all. Such people, he said, must receive extra aid from the others. He finished by stressing that Ikhbal Khan and Yakub Sher must not speak about their good fortune to anyone else, for they would then wish the same privilege.

"What thought on this does Bahadur Ali, the wazir, have?" the Kandit headman asked, turning to the governor.

"I say, what the sahib wills, you do."

To both men, Brodie explained in Hindustani that Shigo and Wali would accompany them to their villages to take care of the older people and give them all medicines and lotions for the sickness. But now he would protect them and their young men to enable them to care for the others. One by one, the eight men left the feast to have their innoculation of the chicken-pox vaccine Brodie had brought from Gilgit.

"What was all that about?" Cready-Smythe demanded.

"Roll your sleeve up," Brodie ordered, filling his syringe from a sealed vial.

"Only if you reveal what that brew is."

"Chicken-pox—and you'll be grateful for it where we're going."

Brodie thanked the wazir, then talked him into arranging to put twenty men of the Gilgit Scouts at their disposal for a week. Bahadur Ali complied willingly, for he was old enough to remember, often with regret, the days when British rule kept the whole North-West Frontier quiet. Next, Brodie called Shigo and Wali into the lab to brief them. Already, he had immunized both of them; now he explained he would give them both samples of the filtered virus which they would empty into drinking water at both villages; they need only infect one person and he would do the rest. But nobody must move from the villages after they had spread the virus. They would send word to Runghar village about the sickness and tell the headman to pass this message to the shepherds who must keep clear of the stricken villages. "Very ingenious, Paul," Cready-Smythe murmured, approvingly. "But will it work?"

Before the feasting stopped in the small hours, they put the two Hunza retainers and the ten men from the northern villages on the road. That morning, a helicopter brought a Gilgit Scouts lieutenant into Baltit, and Brodie briefed him about his role. Now, they only had to wait for news of the outbreaks and that came two days later, brought to them by Bahadur Ali who had received a phone message from Pasu.

Brodie had revealed nothing of his scheme to Shane who would never have consented to using people as guinea-pigs, especially for Cready-Smythe's reasons of state. When they had official news of the outbreaks, he tried to persuade her to stay in Hunza and let him handle them alone. She refused point-blank. What if the virus had changed and he went down with it? So, all three loaded their gear on ponies and began the long trek through the Hunza and Chapursan gorges, reaching Kandit on the second day. There, they left Shane and Wali to cope and pressed forward to Sherkut where Shigo had everything in hand. He also had half a dozen Gilgit Scouts, men of his old unit whom Brodie had immunized; they had hidden their uniforms and were helping to nurse the sick villagers.

"How long before word gets across the border?" Cready-Smythe asked.

"If it does, a day—two at the most."

"That gives us time to have a look at what's the other side of the frontier," Cready-Smythe said.

Since they would probably have to climb or traverse glacier ice, they left their ponies in the village and took only rucksacks. They went through Runghar, then struggled upwards to a track high above the river that ran for miles; at one time, it had brought traders into India from Afghanistan and Russian Turkestan through the Irshad Pass; but now, nothing moved along it, and the rope and plank bridges across the small ravines had perished; Brodie and Cready-Smythe had to scramble across small torrents of freezing glacier water or tack upwards and cross the glacier ice. On the other side of the gorge, they twice caught a flash of sunlight off a rifle or field-glasses, and Brodie knew the Gilgit Scouts lieutenant had followed his orders. He rejected Cready-Smythe's proposal to go to the pass, knowing the Russians and Afghans would be watching it; instead, they trudged across the tongue of the Yashkuk Glacier and climbed for three solid hours, hand over foot, up a steep ridge to where they had a view commanding the pass. From there, they could also survey the highest tableland in the world, the Pamirs. Lying behind the ridge, Brodie spread his map. He had no difficulty orientating it, for in China to the north-east lay Mustagh Ata, the ice mountain Cready-Smythe had joked about conquering, and just beyond it, higher still, Kungur Mountain, all of 25,400 feet. Almost due north, but across Afghanistan's northern frontier with Russia, stood two more immense, ice-riven peaks,

Mount Lenin and Mount Communism, almost as high as Kungur. Cready-Smythe pointed to an area almost midway between the four great mountains. "It must be over there," he said.

"Don't be fooled by the light into thinking it's just up the road," Brodie said. "There's twenty miles of Afghanistan to cross, then those mountains on the Russian side. It's a wilderness."

It seemed just that, this vast range of snow-capped peaks protruding out of great glaciers and separated by deep valleys. They both realized that even in summer they could meet blizzards of snow followed by dust-storms, that the temperature could touch 120 degrees Fahrenheit in the shade during the day and plummet to thirty degrees below zero during the nights.

"It's no more than fifty miles from the northern border," Cready-Smythe said.

"With a Soviet lookout post on every second hill and reconnaissance aircraft flying overhead all the time."

A voice came from behind them. "It can be crossed on foot," it said. They looked round to find a man dressed like an Afghan tribesman in coiled turban, long shirt, baggy trousers and leather sandals; as Brodie stared, two other men appeared from behind a pile of rubble.

"Ahmed!" Cready-Smythe cried, but the man he addressed put a finger to his mouth warning that sound carried far in these valleys. Cready-Smythe turned to Brodie and whispered, "This is Ahmed, and his two henchmen, Ayub and Abdul—but they're not real names for you-know-what reason."

Brodie scrutinized them, wondering how they had traversed that great glacier above them and manoeuvred behind them without dislodging a single stone. They had the slate-blue eyes and hawkish faces of Pathans, yet as he gazed, he had the feeling he had met these men before. Catching Cready-Smythe's grin, he realized where. Ahmed was the elegant, cultured man he had met in Delhi, the person who had probably saved his life; his companions had acted as servants at the villa. So, his former boss had recruited Afghans—most likely among the Mujahideen resistance fighters—to help his mission.

"We saw you both come up the valley from the other side of the Irshad Pass," Ahmed said.

Cready-Smythe explained what they had done and suggested the Afghans cross to their own side of the frontier in case they got caught up in any fighting.

"We'll keep a lookout for your visitors," Ahmed said, softly. He told them they had reconnoitred a route across Afghanistan and a secret pass over the frontier into the Soviet Union; he and his two companions had even explored twenty miles of the Pamirs between the Afghan corridor and the Oksu Valley road. No-one had challenged them, but they spotted observation posts on the hills and several Red Army units as well as MIGs and helicopters flying down the valley into Afghanistan. In the Bam-i-Dunya (roof of the world) they had mostly met Tajik farmers and the nomadic Kara-Kirghiz herdsmen grazing their sheep and goats. "But if you make the journey, you must march at night because of the troops and the heat," he said. Taking their map, he showed their line of march from the pass before them down to the Agsu River and west along its valley to a point near the Urtabal Pass between Afghanistan and Russia. But once across the border, they would have to avoid the valleys and take to the mountains, otherwise they would be caught. They shared their midday rations with the Afghans who then disappeared round the flank of the hill and over the glacier as silently as they had come.

"Ahmed's a university lecturer in geology in Kabul," Cready-Smythe said. "His brother was also in the Mujahideen until he was killed by a Russian booby-trap bomb. Ahmed has sworn to revenge him a hundred times."

"And the others?"

"Believe it or not, his former students."

"Are they going with you?"

"If there's no other way."

Across the river gorge, someone flashed a mirror their way; a few minutes later, they heard the staccato rattle of a helicopter flying out of the Agsu Valley and along the tributary leading to the pass in front of them; Brodie put his field glasses on the single-screw machine, picking out the Russian markings and number, watching until it disappeared into the valley. Quarter of an hour later, it rose, banked right and headed north-east along the line Ahmed had traced on their map. Another hour went by before they spied a group of six men on ponies coming into sight on the pass. Now, they dared not use field glasses in case a reflection alerted the riders. They kept track of the group until it vanished into the river gorge below them. Cready-Smythe turned on his side to address Brodie. "You were right. They've come to have a look."

Giving the six men an hour's start, they shouldered their packs and set a course for Sherkut. Half-way down the hill, a Gilgit Scouts naik (corporal) met them with a parade-ground salute. He had orders to escort them to Sherkut, but they must detour round Runghar where the strangers had left one of theirs with a radio set at the gorge entrance. It meant an hour's climb in the burning heat; and at Sherkut, they had to make yet another flanking movement to avoid a second lookout man. They decided to stay on the hillside above the village and found a ridge from which they could watch the four-man team as they toured the village with Ikhbal Khan. When they had made the rounds, their leader left his three remaining men to help treat the villagers and began to look closely at the place; he peered in various corners, paying particular attention to a small lake bled off the Chapursan River; he then did what Brodie had witnessed Dettwiler do at Runghar, walk slowly along the riverbank, inspecting the shingle and examining an area under willows and poplars on the bank.

Brodie beckoned Cready-Smythe to follow him downhill, keeping out of the lookout's line of vision. They entered the headman's house where Shigo and two of the Gilgit Scouts had hidden; Brodie whispered an order for the Scouts to round up the three men in the village and the two men with radio receivers and transmitters in the gorges. He and Cready-Smythe took post by the village entrance to wait for the group leader. As he approached, Brodie saw that under his bush hat he looked nothing like Dettwiler. He had a broad face, green eyes like glacier ice and a short, stocky body. However, he wore much the same garb, a quilted anorak open over a bush shirt, and trousers tucked into leather boots. On spotting them, he concealed his surprise well. "Hallo," he greeted them in English. "I'm Dr Bolanz."

Brodie gave neither his own name nor Cready-Smythe's. He said, "What were you looking for?"

"Looking for?"

"Along by the riverbank."

Dr Bolanz's green eyes shifted from one to the other man. "I was looking for something to suggest why chicken-pox and shingles should suddenly strike a whole village," he murmured.

"Where have you come from?"

Bolanz paused. "We're part of a Red Cross unit helping to treat casualties on the Afghan side. Someone came to say they had a serious epidemic in this village and another one down the river, so we came to see what help we could offer."

"Can we see your papers?" Brodie demanded.

Bolanz drew himself up. "Do you not believe me?" he snapped.

"We would like to examine your papers," Cready-Smythe said.

"If you tell me who you are and what authority you have," Bolanz replied.

"We have authority from the Pakistani political agent at Gilgit and a detachment of Gilgit Scouts to enforce that authority," Cready-Smythe declared.

Bolanz met this with a shrug. From an anorak pocket, he produced his passport and a Red Cross card bearing his name and his assignment to the Red Cross organization operating in Afghanistan. Cready-Smythe passed both documents to Brodie, who studied them. Dr Ernst Wolfgang Bolanz had an Austrian passport, issued in Vienna, showing him to be a doctor of medicine, aged thirty-four, with an address in the Hernalser Hauptstrasse which, if Brodie remembered rightly, ran for several miles. Had this man fallen on an ordinary official, these papers would have passed scrutiny and taken him anywhere. It shook him visibly when Brodie pocketed the passport and Red Cross card and said, "I am afraid we shall have to verify this identity."

"But why?" Bolanz shouted, angrily.

"Spies cross this frontier every day, and you and your men could be spies," Brodie said, blandly. "These papers may be a cover for your real activities."

"That's absurd."

"You have crossed the frontier without legal permission," Brodie said. "Therefore, you have broken Pakistani law. If you have done this in good faith as you claim, and your embassy in Rawalpindi can confirm your identity and your Red Cross post and vouch for you, then there's no need to worry about this formality."

Bolanz blustered and protested, but they escorted him to the village square where the Gilgit Scouts lieutenant had lined up the other five men. Two had Swedish passports, two had Finnish passports and the fifth produced a Portuguese passport. Their short-wave radio equipment was Japanese and their drugs and medical gear had American, British and West German stamps. From what the Scouts said, they had not had the time or opportunity to use their radios before being captured. Within an hour they had loaded their own and the Red Cross ponies and set off in convoy along the gorges to Hunza. "I just hope you're right about all this, Paul," Cready-Smythe muttered as they followed the rearguard of the Gilgit Scouts into the river gorge.

"I hope so, too," Brodie said, then grinned at Cready-Smythe. "But if I'm not, at least you're carrying the can for this one as the boss man."

At Kandit, they picked up Shane and Wali. She stared at the six men on ponies and Brodie explained they had come across the frontier like the men they had previously met during the Runghar outbreak. "They were captured by the Gilgit Scouts who are taking them back for questioning," he said, smoothly.

Shane reined her pony alongside Brodie's. "I just can't understand how these two new outbreaks started," she remarked.

"It's got me baffled, too," Brodie said.

"You know what it means," she said. "You and your friend Cready-Smythe will have to give up your nice theory about birds."

"What makes you say that?"

"It's too much of a coincidence that an infected bird can land twice in the same area."

"They're creatures of habit," Brodie replied, then went on, tongue-in-cheek. "Anyway, it could be a sick bird that has been trapped here for the past month."

"Paul, you have an answer for everything."

XIV

BOLANZ AND HIS five men were lodged in the only jail the valley possessed, for rare Hunza wrongdoers went to a labour camp in the Shimsal gorge and had to dig salt. At the wazir's suggestion, the political agent sent one of his staff to interrogate the men as potential spies; but the wily old governor gave Brodie and Cready-Smythe a week to put the six men through their own form of cross-examination and make their own private enquiries. Bolanz would not budge one word from his story; they were a Red Cross group bringing medical aid to a stricken village with the finest humanitarian motives.

"Where were you based in Afghanistan?" Brodie asked.

"We were a mobile unit responsible to Red Cross headquarters in Kabul."

"The name of your superior there?"

"Dr Josef Dettwiler," Bolanz replied. "You can contact him through Kabul."

Brodie gave no indication that he had already met Dettwiler at Runghar; he had no doubt the Russian-backed regime in Afghanistan would uphold this lie, and probably use tough diplomacy or even force to recover their six men. "How did you learn about the epidemic?" he asked.

"I only received the order to report to the villages," Bolanz answered. "Probably one of the natives came over for help. They often did along that border."

"As a doctor, what do you think caused the outbreak in those two isolated villages?"

"Either a carrier—somebody with sub-clinical chicken-pox—or a virus getting the upper hand over a person with reduced resistance."

"What were you looking for along the riverbank?"

"Nothing—I only went for a walk."

Brodie shrugged and looked at Cready-Smythe who went outside to return with a box which he opened and thrust under Bolanz's nose. "It wouldn't be something like this, would it?" For twenty seconds, Bolanz stared at the dead ruff lying in its bed of straw, its scarred breast exposed. That sight had obviously shaken him.

"I don't understand," he stammered. "What has that thing got to do with a shingles outbreak?"

"We thought you might enlighten us about that, since you were looking for a sick bird, weren't you?" the SIS man said.

"Of course not," said Bolanz. "I've never even heard of birds contaminating people with the herpes or varicella viruses," he added, recovering some of his composure.

Day after day, they put these and a hundred other questions to Bolanz and his five men; but they had all rehearsed their parts well. However, the moment they returned to Hunza from the two villages, Cready-Smythe had sat down and drafted a long, coded memo to London, passing through Mankad at Gilgit. Five days later, he was able to face Bolanz with the first of the questions that even he could not evade. "What would you say if I told you we had checked with Red Cross headquarters in Geneva and found that neither a Dr Josef Dettwiler nor a Dr Ernst Wolfgang Bolanz belonged to their organization, or had credentials from it to work in Afghanistan?"

"They are mistaken." Yet, when he read the letter from Geneva confirming what Cready-Smythe had stated, his green eyes looked worried.

"Who exactly are you, Herr Doktor?" Cready-Smythe asked.

"Dr Ernst Bolanz, as my passport proves."

Two days later, Cready-Smythe received a long, coded message from London and again summoned Bolanz to the police inspector's small office where they held their interrogations. "Your story gets stranger and stranger," he murmured. "Listen to this." He read from his message. "Austrian authorities confirm a passport was issued by post to Ernst Wolfgang Bolanz. But a check on the birthdate reveals the said Ernst Wolfgang Bolanz died thirty-two years ago, aged three, and is buried in Hernalser Friedhof with his parents, who ran a grocer's shop in the Seventh District." Cready-Smythe paused to fix Bolanz with his blue eyes. "Well, what do you make of all that, Herr Doktor?"

"It is a coincidence."

"Another coincidence—little Ernst would have been about your age had he lived," Cready-Smythe went on, smoothly. "However, I suppose the Austrian consul in Rawalpindi will help us to clear up this mystery."

Bolanz got to his feet. "I shall not go to Rawalpindi. I demand to be released immediately with my orderlies."

"You'll have a fair trial before a military tribunal which will probably decide either to shoot you for spying, or jail you and your men for thirty years," Cready-Smythe drawled. "It should cause quite a sensation when the world press gets hold of the story, don't you think, Paul?"

"Nobody can prove anything," Bolanz cried, but much of his poise had gone.

"If you're not going to help, perhaps one of your men can," Cready-Smythe continued. "This man, Nils Linqvist, for instance. You see, a Nils Linqvist of the same birthdate and address died fifteen years ago and is buried in his native town of Angelholm."

Cready-Smythe turned to Brodie, wide-eyed with mock astonishment. "Full of coincidences, this story," he said. "We'll probably find the Finnish and Portuguese orderlies are dead, too."

Brodie nodded. They both knew well that those passports had been procured through various embassies in the countries concerned, then altered in minor details; someone had zealously scrutinized public records offices and headstones to compile case-histories of dead people then use this information to apply for official passports, knowing that overworked passport offices could not make physical checks of applicants.

"Have another go at Linqvist," Brodie suggested when they had taken Bolanz away.

For two whole days, they had cross-questioned the blond and burly orderly without seeing him flinch. But now, no sooner had he sat down than Cready-Smythe declared he and the others were going to the Pakistani capital the next day to be put on trial for spying. "We now have clear evidence that all six of you have been conducting an espionage campaign," the SIS man said, waving the Swedish passport. "Do you know who Nils Linqvist was?" he asked, and when the orderly pointed at himself, went on, "He was a young Swedish architect, just graduated from Stockholm University. Fifteen years ago he went with two other young graduates on a ski-ing holiday in Lapland. They picked his body out of an avalanche of snow with the two others." He looked at the orderly, then said, "Of course, your spymasters told you another story about your background when they provided you with this passport, didn't they?"

"I am not a spy," Linqvist said.

"Then tell us why you crossed the frontier and we might place a word with the Pakistani authorities that will cut your sentence from twenty years to maybe one or two years."

"In fact, if he agrees to give truthful evidence, we may persuade them to drop the charges against him altogether," Brodie put in.

Linqvist thought about that for several minutes while the two men watched him. Finally, he said, "I will not give evidence against my compatriots."

"No-one asks you to do that. We just want the truth."

"The truth is my name is Ivan Vasilevich Shirokov and I am a sergeant in the Red Army medical corps. They issued me with this passport and sent me on this mission, and that is all I know."

"Who is Dr Bolanz?"

"I do not know his name. I only met him once before—at a bird sanctuary in the mountains."

Brodie and Cready-Symthe hid their surprise at this disclosure. "Was he a medical officer at this nature reserve, then?"

"I cannot say. I only went there with medical supplies from my unit in Afghanistan."

"Where was this bird sanctuary?"

Shirokov shrugged. "In a valley in the middle of the Pamirs. There's a big lake there. We went in by helicopter, for the roads aren't good."

"What kind of birds were they breeding?"

"I'm not much of a hand at birds—different kinds." He thought for a minute. "Gulls and long-legged birds they kept under a big net by the lake. But they had huts full of other birds. I didn't see much of those."

"Was the sanctuary guarded by soldiers?"

"There's an army unit inside, and a big wire fence all round—but they weren't worried—it's miles from anywhere and hard to get at."

"How long were you there?"

"Two hours—the time to dump our load of medicine and lab equipment and have a bite in the army canteen."

Shirokov could tell them little more about the bird sanctuary. Judging by the information he gave about the buildings, the supplies he had taken and other hints, they had about a dozen or perhaps twice that number of staff to look after the birds; he had counted about sixty or seventy people in the canteen, mostly soldiers. Cready-Smythe cautioned the orderly against revealing to his superior or fellow-soldiers that he had answered questions, especially about the bird sanctuary. As he rose to go, he muttered, "Anyway, I wouldn't like to go there again."

"Why not?" Brodie queried.

"They shot me full of bugs a week before I went and both my arms blew up and I was on my back for two days."

When Shirokov had gone, Cready-Smythe picked up the cassettes, and the tape machine on which he had taped the interrogation. "I've got to get in there and have a look at that bird farm," he said.

Brodie pointed to the cassettes. "At least you now have one or two bargaining counters," he said.

"Somehow I don't think the Russians are going to worry too much about what happens to those six men."

"Not even if Shirokov and Bolanz talk?"

"No," Cready-Smythe said. "They'll claim they're Western stooges reciting an SIS or CIA script."

"You don't think they'll make an attempt to rescue them by force."

"That would incriminate them, and create an international diplomatic incident, and not even the Russians would risk that."

Back in the old palace at Baltit, Cready-Smythe played back the Shirokov tape for Shane's benefit; she listened carefully to the statements the Russian had made about the bird sanctuary, then the SIS man's arguments that they were infecting the birds. "Well, I suppose they could be doing some form of virus experiments with birds," she conceded.

"Shirokov had a whole pharmacopoeia of vaccines," Cready-Smythe said. "What diseases would they be protecting him against?"

Shane thought for a moment or two. "They could give him chicken-pox and a vaccine against the adenoviruses as well as the usual tetanus, anti-typhoid, flu, measles, mumps, polio, smallpox. They might even have given him interferon as a general protection."

"What about diseases that birds carry naturally?"

"There's only one recognized bird disease that's transmitted to humans, and that's psittacosis or ornithosis, and it's carried by parrots, pigeons, canaries, budgies."

Cready-Smythe thumbed in the direction of the clinic and lab. "Can you give me what you think Shirokov got?" he asked.

"I'd have to order a whole batch of vaccines from Pindi," she replied.

"As soon as you can then, Madam the doctor."

Brodie looked at his old chief. "So, you're really serious about getting into that bird farm."

"I've no option, if we want to find out what they're really doing to those birds."

Brodie shook his head. "It's crazy enough to think you can reach the place over that wilderness of mountains—but it's suicide to poke your nose into that camp." Brodie lit himself a cigarette and dragged deeply on it. "We only mentioned birds and they set a murder squad on us in Delhi, and you're going to walk right into it."

"I've got to, Paul, before they disband that unit and move away from the frontier to a safer area."

"Why the rush?"

"They'll know by now we've captured Bolanz, Shirokov and the others, and they must assume they've given us some information."

"But they'll think they're safe where they are in that bird farm," Brodie objected. "All they have to do is strengthen the guard." He pointed at the cassettes, and the papers Cready-Smythe carried with him wherever he went. "Take back what you've got to London and forget the heroics."

Cready-Smythe shook his head. "I've taken the assignment." His bare arm swung in a half-circle, embracing the lush, tree-stippled valley and the awesome barrier of mountains, their summits outlined in brilliant white against the azure sky. He looked at them both. "If I don't go soon, this place will get into my system and I'll feel like doing what you did—staying on." He excused himself, saying he was going to have Shigo fill the water tank and have a shower before dinner.

"He's an idiot," Brodie said when Cready-Smythe had disappeared. "Letting himself in for a suicide mission like this when he could easily have sent somebody else."

"Somebody like you," Shane said, pointedly.

"He always took his share of risk." Brodie gave her a worried look. "He believes this could be his last run—that he won't come back."

"And he still wants to drag you with him . . ."

"He hasn't said that."

"No, but he knows you too well," Shane said. "He knows you'll sit here dying a thousand deaths wondering what's happening to him, and blaming yourself if anything does." Shane went inside to write an order for the vaccines and medicines she did not possess and sent Shigo down the hill to phone Gilgit and have them put on the next helicopter flight. Returning to the terrace, she noticed in her absence Brodie had smoked two more cigarettes and was replaying one of the tapes of their various sessions with the six prisoners. Why did that wretched spymaster have to intrude on their lives with his devious games? However, Shane recognized the psychological attachment Paul had for Cready-Smythe and noticed the SIS chief had the same sort of feeling for his former agent, even deferring to him, and often depending on him and his experience; this emotional link stemmed from their mutual respect as well as the life-and-death situations they had faced together. Now, aware of Paul's dilemma, she choked back the oath on her tongue about Cready-Smythe, then went and put an arm round Brodie and surprised him by kissing him on the lips.

XV

JUST AFTER MIDNIGHT, Shigo padded into their room to wake them and whisper that the wazir had brought four strangers to see them. Brodie rose and slipped into warm clothing against the brittle cold that gripped the valley after sunset; Bahadur Ali entered to shake his hand and apologize for disturbing his night. "They have a laissez-passer from the provincial governor," he whispered. Without explaining who the visitors were, he explained they had come to Pasu by helicopter and Wali, his seneschal, had to go through the gorge and conduct them to the capital. They had brought a package for Dr Kingslake. Brodie stepped on to the terrace where he could only make out the dark shapes of the four people. A moon was rising behind Rakaposhi backlighting its splintered silhouette, but leaving the valley in darkness. He approached the group. "What can we do for you?" he asked.

"We are come to see Professor Kingslake," a woman's voice said in tinkling English that struck some memory chord. He called them inside where Shigo had lit a pressure-lamp and was heaping scrubwood on their open fire. In the glow, Brodie recognized the woman, despite the fur hood she wore. It was Dr Huang Ch'ing-hua from the WHO regional office in Delhi. With her stood three men, also Chinese, in thick poshteens, fur hats and felt trousers. "We did not wish to be seen, therefore we travelled by night," Dr Huang said. "We are sorry to wake you." She no longer looked or sounded like the diffident WHO official and Brodie assumed that she had some connection with the state security service.

By now, Shane had pulled on slacks and shoes and her sheepskin jacket and had come to join them. Dr Huang first introduced her three companions. Dr Liu Ho-san was from the Sinkiang health department, Dr Wang Tsi-shai and Sheng Ting-ya were from the defence department in Peking. Brodie studied the two men from the Chinese capital; Wang had a full, smooth face, thick lips and dark eyes capped by thick eyebrows and might have passed for a young edition of Mao Tse-tung; on the other hand, Sheng could have passed for a European, for he looked as aristocratic as Cready-Smythe, and before Communism his family head would have worn a mandarin's robes and long fingernails. Counter-espionage men, Brodie thought. Dr Liu might be one of their technical advisers. Brodie turned to Shigo. "Go and wake Smythe-sahib," he ordered.

They waited until Cready-Smythe appeared, in a long, wool-lined coat, grumbling about losing sleep and the biting cold. Brodie did the introductions, then said to Dr Huang, "You'd better tell us what it's all about."

"This," she said, pointing to a small box Dr Liu carried. They all watched him open it and pull out the bird. Even in the lamplight, they identified it straightaway as a ruff, just like the one Cready-Smythe had received from Africa via London. "It was trapped on the edge of the Kun Lun Mountains," Dr Huang explained. "It was dying," she went on.

"Did it infect anyone?" Cready-Smythe asked.

She nodded. "A small community of jade miners south of Khotan suffered from throat and chest infections."

"Did they get what we call Pink-eye?" Brodie queried.

"Yes," Dr Huang said. "When I heard this, I had Dr Liu take throat swabs and analyse the virus. It was an adenovirus type Three."

"The kind of virus carried by some birds and other creatures," Dr Liu put in.

"We have never seen this disease in that area before," Dr Huang said. "We would not have connected it with the outbreaks in India if Dr Kingslake had not given her lecture in Delhi." She gave a slight bob of her head towards Shane. "I reported all this to our authorities and we asked permission to come and meet you. That is all."

"Why Dr Kingslake?" Brodie asked.

"Because she is first to suggest the theory birds are carrying diseases, and we are thinking she has more information."

"No, we have no more information than we gave in Delhi," Brodie answered, glancing at Cready-Smythe and then at the dead bird in Dr Liu's hands. Taking the bird from the Chinese, the SIS man moved over to the pressure-lamp, calling Brodie across to study it; they noted the surgical scars under its breast, identical with the marks on their own bird. Cready-Smythe whispered, "Can we trust them, do you think, Paul?"

"That's up to you."

"Didn't Confucius once say the enemy of your enemy is your friend?"

"Anyway, they have a right to know what is happening to these birds."

At that, Cready-Smythe handed the bird back and disappeared towards his room. Ten minutes later he returned with his file, carefully edited. Emphasizing he was showing them confidential material, he produced his map and several pictures and delivered a shorter version of what facts they had on the bird sanctuary. Brodie listened, remembering the night in the villa when he had spotted the Chinese emerging from his interview with the SIS man, and then the allusions to climbing the Mustagh Ata. He understood his former intelligence chief only too well to imagine he had decided on the spur of the moment to reveal his top-secret material; somehow, he or someone higher up had made a deal with the People's Republic of China which had a pathological xenophobia about the Russians who reciprocated the feeling; Brodie knew the spy world well enough to realize this was a working partnership.

Both Chinese security men pored over the satellite pictures and the matching maps. "It would be very simple to destroy this place," Wang murmured.

"Then you would never find out what they had been doing there," Cready-Smythe objected.

"And without proof of what they're up to, they can build another camp like that in a week and start again elsewhere," Brodie put in. Sheng nodded acknowledgement and agreement.

"Anyway, if they are infecting birds as you claim, it might be very dangerous to destroy the camp," Shane protested. "If you bomb that place and release those birds, they might cause a lot of deaths by disseminating strange viruses among unprotected people."

"I agree with Dr Kingslake," Dr Huang said. "Just imagine if some of those birds were carrying lethal viruses like smallpox, or a bacillus like bubonic or pneumonic plague. Unless people were prepared by vaccination we would have massive epidemics."

"But if the people who infected the birds had already innoculated their populations, they would have a great advantage in the event of a war," Cready-Smythe murmured.

"Exactly what we thought," Sheng said.

By now, everyone had sat down on the primitive chairs and stools in the room and, since the fire had warmed the atmosphere, the visitors had removed their mountain clothing. Shigo made them tea, boiling it with milk and salt, Hunza-fashion; as they tasted it, the Chinese grimaced and stared at each other, but they swallowed it politely and courageously. Wang and Sheng were studying the maps and pictures. Sheng turned to Cready-Smythe and Brodie. "But this place lies no more than thirty miles from our Sinkiang frontier."

"They had to place it near their own frontiers to save them from infecting their own population and, at the same time, giving themselves away."

"It would be possible to drop people either by helicopter or parachute at night in the area," Wang suggested.

Brodie rejected this. "You'd be picked up by radar, they'd be waiting for us and we'd lose the surprise element and all chance of getting into the camp." Unconsciously, he had used the word "we" which was not lost on Cready-Smythe or Shane.

"What do you think's the best plan, Paul?" the SIS man asked.

"Can the Chinese get us across the frontier on foot—opposite the camp?" He pointed to an area along the Sino-Soviet frontier about fifty miles into China. "That'll give us between twenty and thirty miles of hiking to do."

For several minutes both Chinese security men studied the map, mumbling and tongue-clicking at each other before Sheng nodded. "West of Tashkurgan there is peak over eighteen thousand feet high. One slope is not well-guarded."

"We can transport weapons and bombs," Wang put in.

"No," Cready-Smythe snapped. "Too risky and you might give the game away. Anyway, I don't like guns and bombs." He tapped his forehead. "We use this," he said.

"Have we any friends on the other side?" Brodie queried.

"We can arrange contacts," Sheng replied.

"But we're not going to footslog it over those mountains both ways," Cready-Smythe exclaimed.

"No," Brodie said. "The way I see it, we walk in and they bring us out."

"How?"

"They can airlift us," Brodie said. Briefly, he explained his scheme and the Chinese nodded approval; even his old boss congratulated him on its ingenuity, saying if they had to get into the camp and discover its secrets, the plan seemed the only way that gave them an even chance of escaping. For no-one doubted the risks or the fact the Russians would do everything to destroy them and keep their operation to themselves. As Brodie detailed his project, all the Chinese except Dr Liu took notes, filling their small memo-pads with ideograms. When they had finished, Dr Huang flashed a smile at Cready-Smythe. "I should like permission to accompany you, if I may," she said.

"Why?"

"To see with my own eyes."

"It will be too tough."

"Please," she pleaded. "I am strong."

"All right," Cready-Smythe said, finally. "We shall be pleased to have you with us, Dr Huang."

Shane gave the Chinese woman doctor instructions about the vaccines and sera to use on herself and her companions. When they had finished their discussions, they declined Shigo's offer of more Hunza tea and, at four o'clock, took their leave.

Next day, Cready-Smythe went down to Karimabad to collect his mail and several bits of equipment from the Gilgit helicopter. He climbed the hill with a bulky parcel for Shane, and he and Brodie watched as she opened it to produce two dozen phials, all labelled. His eyes wide with surprise and apprehension, Cready-Smythe pointed to the medicaments. "You're not going to shoot that lot into me," he groaned.

"No, there are four lots."

"Four lots!" both men got out at the same time.

Shane pointed to them, then to herself and lastly to Shigo. She smiled at Brodie. "Don't forget I was in at the beginning, so I want to be in at the end."

"Shane, you can't do it," Brodie said. "It'll be tough for us."

"If Dr Huang can stand the trip, I can," she came back. "Anyway, I'm not going to sit here all alone wondering whether you're alive or dead."

XVI

CREADY-SMYTHE REFUSED THE Chinese offer to fly them from Hunza into Sinkiang by helicopter; they must look like some small mountaineering party, at least until they crossed the Mintaka Pass into China. They had kitted themselves out with climbing gear, warm clothing and rations for two weeks which they loaded on ponies. Even now, the middle of August, they would need their sheepskins and felt trousers at nights. As well as Shigo, they had brought Wali who had volunteered with the wazir's blessing. Brodie had lost count of the times he had slogged through the Hunza River gorges which headed up into the pass; on Pasu glacier they had to shoot one of their pack ponies which slipped and broke a leg, and this made much heavier weather of the Mintaka which lay at 15,600 feet. It seemed interminable, one long upward haul leading into another until even at midday on the third day their breath condensed in white puffs and their ponies picked their way through the bones of those that had died on the pass; as they came in sight of the Pamirs on the Chinese side, the men dismounted and led their animals over the Pass of a Thousand Ibex. A long, zig-zag descent over a rock-strewn valley wedged between black, ice-clad mountains, took them to Mintaka Karaul, the Chinese frontier post. Here, travellers could languish several days waiting for clearance; but the Chinese civil servant, in blue Mao tunic, gave their papers one glance and waved them past the guards.

When they broke out of the pass into grazing land, they made camp. Further down the green valley, they spied herds of sheep and goats and the yurts (round, felt tents) of Kirghiz shepherds. Shigo and Wali rode down and returned with two jars of goat-milk and half a sheep which they cut up expertly and grilled over a wood fire. As they finished eating, two Kirghiz shepherds approached their camp on yaks, screwing round faces and slant eyes into smiles and making a clasped-hands Indian greeting.

"They are wishing to know where we are going," Shigo said.

"Tell them we're climbing Mustagh Ata," Cready-Smythe grunted.

At this, the Kirghiz pair looked grave, and the senior man muttered something. Shigo grinned at Cready-Smythe. "He is saying to take our headstones with us."

Cready-Smythe produced a handful of yuan notes and Wali offered two bottles of Hunza beer to repay the Kirghiz hospitality. Having voiced their thanks, they trotted off, balancing on the bare backs of their small yaks.

"I don't trust the Kirghiz," Cready-Smythe murmured to Brodie.

"Why single out them?" Brodie replied, sarcastically, knowing the SIS man trusted nobody, not even his own aristocratic family; indeed, he doubted if his wife and two sons had rumbled the fact that he did not earn his money as a Lloyds insurance underwriter.

"Don't you think we should leave Shane in China?" Cready-Smythe said.

"I suggested that to her and she refused."

"You know what the Russians do with spies," the SIS man went on.

"I didn't think you did when you used to hand out missions."

"But why does she want to come?"

"Why? Because we both think medicine should be a healing art and not some biological toy used for mass murder. So, don't think we're on Her Majesty's secret service—you're the only one."

Next day, they made a wide sweep round Tashkurgan. Its primitive bazaar with oriental stalls, its caravans and tented camps, even its scalloped old fort housed dozens of part-time Soviet spies who operated along a couple of hundred miles of this vague and undefined frontier. Several miles above the town, they left the Yarkand River valley and started climbing west along one of its tributaries. An hour before sunset, they arrived within three miles of the Russian frontier, in a deep cleft of the mountain, at the spot the two Chinese security men had designated as a rendezvous. A small tamarisk grove camouflaged them and broke the fierce wind that funnelled along the valley. When they had dumped their bags, Cready-Smythe called them together; they were not making camp since the Chinese would meet them two hours after sunset and escort them across the frontier; once there, they must march only at night and lie up during the day; therefore, they would leave the ponies here and take only what they could carry on their backs. He looked at all four of them in turn. "I should tell you that any of us who is injured or cannot march must be left to the Russians," he said. Each of them nodded.

They could not light a fire, but heated their tinned-meat rations over two gas burners and ate as the sun went off the valley, playing for quarter of an hour on the ice ridges of Mustagh Ata and Kungur to their left then plunging them into darkness, broken only by starlight. Brodie and Shane could hardly believe it, but as they packed their rucksacks, snow began to fall in flurries though the wind swept it downhill where it collected in drifts.

An hour before midnight, Sheng crept into their camp with two other Chinese who took charge of their ponies. In single file, they followed the shadowy silhouette of Sheng along the cleft, then began to pick their way upwards. Shigo kept ahead of Shane, helping her over the roughest parts while Brodie followed closely behind her, ready to catch her if she stumbled. Every half-hour they rested for five minutes; during one pause, Sheng sucked on an unlit cigarette and told them in muted tones that Dr Huang and Wang had already crossed the frontier and were waiting for them. Brodie wondered how, for he knew that at least a hundred yards separated the high, barbed-wire fences marking the border, and the Russians had probably electrified their wire as well as stationing troops in watch-towers.

An hour later, he found out. How the Chinese had accomplished it without discovery, he never knew; but somehow, they had managed to tunnel through the hard rock of the mountain from thirty yards behind their own wire to fifty yards beyond the Soviet frontier. When they had crawled through the first fifty yards on hands and knees, Brodie realized a subterranean stream had done some of the work, gouging a long cavern out of the rocks before working downwards and leaving a dry tunnel large enough for the miners to store the debris from their drilling operation. In this cavern beneath the no-man's-land, Cready-Smythe split them into two parties; he and Sheng would lead with Wali, keeping at twenty-yard intervals; Brodie, Shane and Shigo would follow, just within sight of Wali, their last man; that way, if they met a Soviet patrol, at least some of them would have the chance to escape.

A sickle moon had risen, shedding enough light to enable them to spot shadow and movement. For an hour they continued along the mountainside, having to descend every now and again to ford torrents spilling towards the anonymous tributary of the Balgyn River, one of those filling the two lakes where their bird sanctuary lay. Suddenly, Brodie who was leading the second party, noticed Wali disappear; he was groping forward when a hand reached out to grab his arm. Sheng pointed down the sharp ridge where Wali had gone. "There is cave," he whispered through his cupped hand. On reaching the spot, Brodie saw the others had already foregathered in the middle of the deep grotto. It was well chosen, for its dogleg shape would hide them from anyone in or across the valley.

Incongruously, with the solemnity of some society hostess, Dr Huang had prepared to receive them, offering a choice of China tea, or rice wine in tiny cups. She and Wang had lit a gas burner to take the dead chill off the cave, for outside the temperature had fallen well below zero; they had made soup of rice and vegetables which they served in mugs. Sheng joined them and he, Cready-Smythe and Brodie compared notes about their next day's march; they decided to strike north-west until they hit the upper reaches of the Balgyn River then follow this, though remaining on the high crests, to the lake.

Brodie observed Sheng seemed to have taken charge of the three Chinese; Dr Huang and Wang listened with inclined heads as he issued instructions in staccato, tinkling phrases without ever changing his impassive, mandarin expression. Wherever he went, he slung his knapsack over his back—even when he slipped outside to relieve himself. Shigo was also watching this little act. He approached Brodie to whisper, "Paul-sahib, they have guns, and Wang has much . . ." Not knowing the word, Shigo mimed a bundle of explosives and a big bang. Neither Cready-Smythe nor Brodie ever carried firearms and they had warned the Chinese not to bring any; but Sheng obviously intended to make good his idea of destroying the camp. When Brodie mentioned the facts to Cready-Smythe he merely shrugged and said he had no authority over them.

All that day they remained in their cave. It gave them a grim foretaste of summer weather on the roof of the world. Until sunrise, they had shivered with the cold, beating their frozen hands and stamping their feet to keep their circulation going, and huddling together for comfort; but two hours after dawn, even in that deep grotto, the heat became stifling; melting snow had turned the streams into torrents and their spray steamed and sizzled on the rocks when a few hours ago it had frozen on their faces, their clothing, their packs and formed icicles. Below them, through the shimmering heat, they sighted a valley between the mountains and they reckoned that down there, the thermometer must be registering something like a hundred and fifty degrees Fahrenheit in the shade, even at ten thousand feet. Only on the highest peaks did snow and ice stick; everywhere else, it was melting to feed the torrents that gouged deep clefts, in the mountains.

They had done well deciding to march at night, for they would certainly have been spotted from the air. Most of that day, their region of the Pamirs reverberated with sonic bangs as MIG fighters and fighter-bombers flew from northern bases into Afghanistan; a dozen helicopters clattered along the Oksu Valley, no more than twenty miles away, carrying supplies and troops. Had the Chinese attempted to airlift them into this area of Soviet Tajikstan, they would have lasted an hour at the most. In the late afternoon, the wind backed and blew from the east, veiling the whole landscape with a thick haze of dust from the Takla Makan desert in Sinkiang across the Chinese border; since this cut their visibility to no more than two hundred yards, it meant they could move around the cave without the risk of being spotted.

That night, between eleven o'clock and five, they covered just eleven miles, for the moon had set and they had to feel every yard of their route over the scree-bound flank of the mountain range. If the wind had dropped, they still had to battle against bone-chilling cold and the tenuous, lifeless air at nearly twelve thousand feet. When they inched upwards to avoid the deeper ravines, they had to stop to allow the two women and Wang to rest for a minute in every five. Behind him, in the dead stillness, Brodie could hear Shane breathing in rapid, lung-straining spurts and, although drained himself, he contrived to pull her over the steepest terrain with the rope. As always, his left leg was going numb and leaden from the old compound fracture, and the plastic-surgery patches on his face felt dead as though all circulation had ceased. Far below them, in the valley, they now saw lights, presumably from the mud-brick and thatch dwellings of Tajik peasant farmers. All that night they encountered only one patch of level ground and Sheng and Cready-Smythe refused to risk traversing it; two yurts lay at one end, shedding their light on the herd of sheep and goats bedded there until dawn. "They're Kirghiz and they'll have pi-dogs and give us away," Brodie whispered to Shane when she dumped herself down and grumbled about having to scale another ridge and several more ravines.

Sheng obviously had some idea where he was leading them, for he stopped every half hour to study his own map and a hand-drawn chart. When he stepped up the pace, sending them stumbling over loose rock and piled-up scree, Brodie realized he was trying to locate their rendezvous before first light, which in these mountains came without warning. They missed the place and had to backtrack for half a mile, arriving with less than a quarter of an hour to spare. It was a stone cabin which sat on a gentle slope, overgrown with tussocky grass, scrub and tamarisk and butting against a sheer cliff face. Three of its four walls and part of its roof remained intact. Built from scree and moraine by Kirghiz shepherds to protect them from the freezing winds and blistering sun, it overlooked the valley yet lay hidden against the cliff. Once inside, they risked lighting a gas stove to warm the roofed section. Brodie spent half an hour rubbing Shane's frozen fingers and massaging her chilled and tired feet to restore the circulation. "There's still time to turn back," he said. She shook her head, wearily.

When dawn broke, they could see the Balgyn River in the distance. Twelve miles downstream, it emptied into the main lake where their bird farm sat. But twelve miles across these mountains! In daylight, Brodie glanced around to see how the others had fared after several nights on the march. Dr Huang looked more exhausted than Shane; her face had a drawn, ivory look and it seemed to have shrunk with weariness; she sat cradling her head on her drawn-up knees and left her two companions to break out their chicken-and-rice ration and warm it over a burner. More than twice her age, Shigo and Wali had taken that mountain trek in their stride and were opening tins of beef stew, French beans and frozen chips which they heated on their butane stove. When they had eaten this, they felt much stronger, though Brodie had to spoon-feed Shane, so tired did she seem. He made tea which Cready-Smythe spiked with Scotch from the bottle he carried. Even the three Chinese accepted a splash in their small cups with a bow. Both parties decided to share a watch during the day while the others slept. Brodie made Shane as comfortable as possible on a dry ledge near the wall and she fell asleep straight away in her sleeping-bag; he also found Dr Huang a dry corner; she did not even bother to take off her damp clothing before crawling into her sleeping-bag, tucking her small, dark head into the hood of her anorak and dropping into an exhausted sleep.

"What's your plan when we get there?" Brodie whispered to Cready-Smythe as they smoked a final cigarette.

"Afraid we have to busk this one, Paul . . . take it as it comes. Somehow, we've got to get into that camp and at least one of us has to get out with whatever we can grab in the way of information."

"I don't give much for our chances."

"We've survived worse."

"All right, say we do get out with a whole skin?"

Cready-Smythe produced a map and placed a finger on a spot ten miles or so south of the camp in a deep valley cut by one of the small rivers feeding the Oksu. "It's too small to be marked, but there's a hamlet there called Belkuz—the last rendezvous I made with the Chinese. We head for that and hope the Chinese have the nous to follow your plan and hoik us out of the place."

"Do we have a contact there?"

Cready-Smythe hesitated. "Yes, there is one, but only the Chinese know him and they refuse to endanger his safety by revealing his name."

From the SIS man's cagey attitude, Brodie realized he knew much more than he would ever divulge about the operation. Why would a man who had never taken an unconsidered step now suggest they play the whole of this complicated manoeuvre by ear? Something stank in Brodie's nostrils, and he wondered how much his old boss knew about that camp by the lake. Shigo and Wali had spread sleeping-bags for them in a corner of the cabin. They lay smoking a final cigarette. "Paul," Cready-Smythe whispered, "one of us must get out once we discover what they're up to. If it's you, get the stuff to London. It's vital."

"I'll hand it over to Mankad at Gilgit."

"No—take it yourself."

He left Brodie with the strong presentiment they were walking into some sort of trap, though whether Russian or Chinese he had no idea.

For most of that day they slept. In the late afternoon a thudding wind woke them and they bunched together under the roofed part of the cabin to prepare their meal and pack their rucksacks. Half an hour after the sun slid behind the higher peaks of the Pamirs, they began the last leg of their outward march. Within two miles it started to snow, the wind flinging it into their faces, numbing them, blinding them and cutting their visibility to no more than ten yards. Cready-Smythe relayed word forward to Sheng to halt before they lost each other in the blizzard. Producing a rope, he knotted it at ten-yard intervals, instructing them to tie the knots to their rucksacks so they would keep together. Although the snow did not lie thick, it hindered their progress, for now they had to test each step in case they hit loose scree and caused an avalanche. It soaked through their clothes, adding to their weight; it clung to their climbing boots, tiring everyone, even the Hunza pair. Several times the whole party had to stop and rest, though only for a few minutes at a time. Any longer and the melted snow and their sweat would have frozen on them. Cready-Smythe shared his whisky, and the Chinese drank the rice brandy they had brought to keep their circulation going.

Sheng still led them, and it seemed he was choosing the roughest tracks which switchbacked over the deepest ravines. However, had they climbed to avoid fording the torrents, they would have had to contend with snow and glacier ice. Just after one o'clock, they halted for a briefing by both leaders who stressed that, from now on, they were crossing an area within surveillance by the two Russian lookout posts on the high hills. They would therefore put a hill between them and the nearest post, then descend into the valley. Aerial photos had revealed several caves on one hillside and when they had found these, they would split their forces to lessen the risk of total capture. For an interminable time, they trudged upwards through drifting snow and a wind that knifed through them, filling their lungs with freezing air that had no sustenance and left them gasping.

Brodie shortened the rope between himself and Shane and towed her over the steeper rock outcrops to prevent her from stumbling and falling in the dark. Wali did the same for the petite Chinese doctor who could hardly drag one foot after the other. They could see nothing through the snow. Light, powdery and windblown, it penetrated everything—their anorak hoods, glove hands, climbing boots. It cut their breath and melted in their mouths, open to suck in the vitiated air. But finally, as their long upward detour ended, the snow stopped and some light fell from the brittle stars overhead.

Now, they had to slither downwards, backstopping each other with the rope, testing each foothold under the snow. As they turned north and felt their way round the shoulder of the hill, the faint etched line of the crests against the lighter sky told them they had reached the valley. Great peaks hung sheer over it. Back came a message from Cready-Smythe that, from now on, no-one must make a sound. In dead silence they trudged along the southern flank of the valley, picking their steps, halting every few seconds until the rope went taut and proved the person ahead was still upright and advancing. An hour before dawn, the lakes, then the faint lights from the camp, glimmered into view. Up front, Sheng and Cready-Smythe began to search for the caves; as they climbed a spur, they struck lucky, spotting a waterfall almost directly above the camp. Sheng, who seemed to know the lie of the country, whispered that in these hanging valleys a waterfall often hid a cave. He was right. Behind the fall, they found a cave entrance and plunged through the icy water into shelter. Inside, the cave seeped water from every pore and frozen pools had formed on its floor. But here, nobody would see them; and they had water to brew up and keep them cool during the torrid daytime heat.

They tossed for the cave and Cready-Smythe won, choosing to stay there with Brodie, Shane and Shigo. Before the others left to seek another hiding-place, Brodie had time to whisper to Wali that if the Chinese did anything silly and looked like falling into Russian hands, he must forget heroics and make a run either to rejoin them or cross the frontier. He had decided against giving either of the Hunzas their rendezvous point, aware that Wali and Shigo could lose themselves among the Turki, Tajik and Kirghiz folk in these mountains and somehow trek over the Afghan frontier into their own homeland.

XVII

WHEN THEY HAD gone, Brodie and Cready-Smythe explored their cave which ran backwards for about four yards before kinking and narrowing. There, at least, it had dry patches and they could light their stove without fear that someone on the hilltop observation post would spot the flame. Shigo brewed them strong tea and laced it with home-made apricot brandy and this revived even Shane; somehow, he managed to cook them chupattis, fry the eggs he had carried and serve them breakfast as the sun came over the mountain tops. Their meal finished, Brodie and Cready-Smythe crawled to the cave mouth. Through and round the curtain of water, they could see the two lakes a thousand feet below them and a couple of hundreds yards to their left. "We can use the glasses," Cready-Smythe called, cupping his hand and placing it against Brodie's ear to cut out the sound of the waterfall.

For quarter of an hour, he studied the camp through powerful field-glasses, commenting on what he saw to both Brodie and Shane, who had now joined them. Brodie then took the glasses. He could see why the Russians had chosen the Istky and Oksay Kul lakes to build their secret bird farm, for the valley twisted at the bottom to shut the place off from the view of the main Oksu Valley. It had no pasture to attract Kirghiz herdsmen, only bleak rock and an expanse of salt water.

Swinging his glasses round to survey the path they had taken, he whistled under his breath. A huge outcrop of rock hung above them to their left and, piled above it, a small mountain of scree, slackened and left there by snow and ice. If they had stumbled on that in the dark, they could have started a major landslide. He focused back on the camp. A fifteen-foot high fence surrounded the camp which covered about one mile and was about three hundred yards wide on the edge of the shoe-shaped lake; they had sited the long, prefabricated concrete-and-glass buildings near the lake, and these he took for labs; now he could see clearly the three glass cupolas capping three round, wooden buildings in the style of old-fashioned forts; inside them, he discerned some activity, though he could not tell what kind. He had guessed right about the generator house with its huge reservoir of diesel oil, but he could not see the cables carrying power through the camp and assumed they were buried. They also used propane, for he counted four cylinders, uncovered since they contained highly combustible gas; two lay against a wooden structure, probably the canteen. It looked big enough for no more than fifty people. They could only have a small military detachment, for the long barrack building might house thirty to forty soldiers; however, he guessed those troops would come from the élite KGB border patrol since no country could trust ordinary militia men to keep the sort of secrets they might have here. Their water must come from the stream running beside the camp, for the lake with the high evaporation in this area, had turned salty. No phone wires, but a complex of aerials which meant radio contact with their base. A small hut in the middle of the camp attracted his eye, for a soldier had appeared at the door and he saw two more uniformed men through a window. That must be the guard-room and the armoury.

But the most intriguing feature lay on the camp edge and over part of the lake. Satellite pictures had shown it as a boom, but it was really a great vault of trellis wire, an immense cage for about twenty sea-birds that flew about under it or floated on the water; huge steel hoops fixed the structure to the lake bank and the boom between fifty and a hundred yards out from the water's edge. One by one, they studied this weird construction. "Well, what do you think . . . Paul . . . Dr Kingslake?"

Again, Brodie scrutinized the cage; he counted twenty birds and wondered if the number had any significance. Through his mind, he could hear Asari's quaint Hindi voice and the ribald shouts of the Riswana peasants as he described the birds he had witnessed while fishing. Several of these birds were hovering in the way the old fisherman had mentioned; they had forked tails; and they swooped into the water to catch fish with the synchronous movements that had enthralled Asari. What had he said? His two birds had behaved as one. Staring at these birds, Brodie could see several of them performing like some troupe of trained gulls. He screwed the eyepieces of his binoculars into sharper focus to pick up the scarlet bills, the brown streaks on their wings, their forked tails. "But they're not gulls," he muttered. "They're terns—Caspian terns. Only . . ."

"Only what?" Cready-Smythe prompted.

"Well, it's still summer and Caspian terns should have a black head—but their heads are all grey and streaky, as though these birds thought it was autumn or winter."

"Maybe it's because they're out of their breeding area and the cold nights have given them that impression," Shane remarked.

"No—the temperature and climate wouldn't be enough to fool them," Brodie mused. "Something else has." He could see those birds were fidgety, restless as though preparing for migration, for a long trek over the mountains and down into India and perhaps out to islands in the Indian Ocean. Had something prepared them for unseasonal migration? Had old Asari not spotted those birds, had those two ruffs not fallen sick and been trapped, who would have suspected birds of causing those outbreaks, more so since they were migrating out of season? Who would have connected illnesses like shingles and Pink-eye with birds? But how and why would they use birds like biological missiles? And how could they control their flight?

"What are you thinking, Paul?"

Brodie turned to Cready-Smythe. "That you were right—we'll never know what's going on unless we get into that camp."

All that day, they observed the place, noting its routine, counting its soldiers, the white-coated lab staff and orderlies; at midday and seven o'clock, they watched orderlies carry grain, fish and other feed to the three domed buildings and caught the ensuing flurry of sound and movement; they registered the human feeding-time in two canteen relays between midday and one, and seven and eight. In the afternoon, an MI 10 helicopter arrived with supplies that looked like food, medical equipment and mail. During the day they spotted several MIGs and transport aircraft flying towards the Afghan border. At nine o'clock they saw, with some apprehension, the night patrol emerge from the guardhouse with four Alsatian dogs to patrol the compound fence; just before sunset, as the valley was filling with twilight, the three glass domes suddenly erupted with artificial light, evidently triggered by a single automatic switch. But by dark, blinds had swung into place to black out the illumination.

An hour after nightfall, Wali appeared, to fill three water-bottles at their waterfall then lead them to the cave a hundred feet below, occupied by him and the Chinese. They all looked tired and miserable and they had little to report that the others did not know. In their dry hole they had fried during the broiling heat, and had to retreat to the back for fear of discovery by the observation posts. Without the camouflage of a waterfall, they could not risk using field-glasses, or even crawling to the cave mouth to watch the camp. Brodie and Cready-Smythe explained what they had witnessed.

"That camp must be destroyed," Sheng said.

"Not until we have collected our evidence," Cready-Smythe riposted. "Without that, you'll merely be creating an international incident—and none of us will get out alive."

"These Russian dogs have to be whipped," Wang put it. "It is all they understand."

"There are two platoons of KGB border troops down there and fifty other people," Cready-Smythe said. "If you alert them, you'll have a thousand more on your backs. That wouldn't be very clever."

"Then your suggestion, please?" Sheng said.

"We send a patrol down there later tonight to see how well-guarded the place is and how we can penetrate it."

"Agreed," Sheng said. "Wang and myself are going."

"I'll come with you," Cready-Smythe said to Brodie's astonishment. "We can leave Dr Huang with Mr Brodie and Dr Kingslake." He fixed a rendezvous with the two Chinese state security men for midnight before he, Shane and Brodie felt their way back to their cave. Brodie did not comment on the SIS man's strange decision but he knew he must have powerful reasons for leading a patrol he could easily have delegated. When they had eaten their evening meal, Cready-Smythe donned his warm clothing, blackened his face with wet soil then signed to Brodie to duck under the fall and join him outside. "I couldn't let those two oriental gentlemen go down there on their own and muck things up. But if they land us all in it, you get the women out of here with Shigo and Wali. Shane and Dr Huang will be able to tell some of the tale."

"Where does that leave me?"

"Where you always were, Paul—your own boss." Cready-Smythe put a hand on his shoulder. "You make your own decision."

Brodie watched the long shadow disappear, reflecting that one day, Cready-Smythe would state the unperverted truth. What was the man up to? He had to see. He waited outside the waterfall until Wali brought Dr Huang back and installed her in the cave before calling Shane and Shigo to his side. "I'm going down behind the others," he whispered.

"But that's mad, Paul."

"I've got to see what's there for myself," he muttered. "I'll take Shigo." He embraced Shane, feeling her tremble against him through her thick anorak. "Give us two hours and if we're not back, make your own way back across the frontier with Dr Huang and Wali," he said.

"No," she said. "We stay here."

Brodie did not stop to argue, knowing her as stubborn as himself. Calling softly to Shigo they started downhill, testing each footstep to ensure the ground would not give and send stones or rocks tumbling towards the camp. Brodie headed for the east end of the camp where few buildings stood; he had noticed the patrols did not bother much with this side. There a ridge of high, rocky ground separated the two lakes and they ducked behind this and had soon crossed the most easterly point to the other side. Lying behind the low end of the ridge, they could see all the camp against the sloping lake bank; a few lights glowed in the lab buildings and canteen, and floodlamps lit the roads connecting various sections; at that hour, hardly anything moved except the patrolling troopers with dogs making their round. A hundred yards across the water, they made out the boom and the immense wire cage under which some of the terns were floating, asleep, while others were fidgeting and flying around, occasionally colliding with the trellis.

"Shigo, do you think we can grab a couple of those birds?" he whispered.

"We are waking up everyone, Paul-sahib."

"I know, and the water's freezing."

With his cat's eyes, Shigo nudged him and beckoned across to a point near the entrance gate. Peering over his arm, Brodie could just discern the dog-handlers and several other soldiers converging there; they appeared to have alerted the men in the guard-house, for half a dozen men carrying rifles and machine-pistols were deploying behind the dog-handlers. "They've spotted them," Brodie whispered.

At that moment, a dozen floodlamps flared all round the perimeter fence, lighting the ground behind the camp. Two men broke from behind a pile of rocks and started to sprint up the hill. A rattle of fire from machine pistols and rifles echoed along the valley.

"The two Chinese," Shigo whispered.

"Bloody fools," Brodie said, hoping Cready-Smythe had chosen a good hiding-place and would keep his head down.

One of the Chinese turned and fired a shot, the Russians let off another volley and they saw the Chinese fall forward. His companion turned, raising his hands and walking towards the soldiers emerging from the gate. Now the whole camp had stirred and the great bird-cage over the lake had become a mass of spiralling birds, wakened by the lights and scared by the shooting. Their strident screeching and cawing sounds filled the night. As the light fell on the man who had surrendered, they recognized Sheng; several soldiers were carrying the wounded man into the camp, others escorted Sheng while the remainder fanned out to search the ground around the fence. They did not look very far before a shout went up, and Brodie identified the tall figure of Cready-Smythe, bracketed by two soldiers, who marched him into the camp.

Before closing the gates, the commanding officer posted half a dozen sentries outside to cover the dog-handlers who were searching the area within the camp lights. Obviously, they did not intend to search much beyond the fence during darkness, but Brodie realized they would have all their men out on the hills tomorrow. He had only a few hours in which to act. Within their cage, the terns were still fluttering and complaining loudly. Brodie began to strip off his clothing and Shigo followed his example. Creeping down the bank, they entered the water. It tasted salt and felt so cold, it cut Brodie's breath; they both swam for the boom, moving carefully. When they reached it, Brodie whispered to Shigo to stay outside. He dived under the heavy, metal grid which held the boom together, surfacing on the inside. There, he grasped the boom with one hand and waited, absolutely immobile. After a few minutes, a tern settled nearby. Reaching out, he grabbed it by the head and beak and, before it could squawk, he plunged it underwater and held it there until it drowned. He thrust the dead bird under the grid and it floated to the surface within Shigo's reach. Brodie had intended to capture two birds only, but two more swam innocently up to him and he drowned both and passed them to Shigo.

It took them more than two hours to regain their cave, for they had to make a long detour to avoid the sentries and dog-handlers, climb above the waterfall and come in along the ridge. Shane fell into Brodie's arms. "We heard the shooting and thought they'd caught or killed you both."

He explained what had happened to the Chinese and Cready-Smythe and what they had seen. "They'll search this bit of the hill as soon as the sun comes up," he said. "About two hours," he added, looking at his watch.

"What can we do?" she asked.

"It's no good trying to find another hiding-place," he said. "They've got too many men they can call on and they'll catch us sooner or later."

"We can make a run for it now."

"That's what I was going to suggest you should do—with Wali to take you both out," Brodie said. He pointed to the three dead terns. "You can take one of these birds with you as evidence."

"But what about you?" Shane cried.

"I've got an idea—if Shigo agrees to stay with me." When Shigo nodded, Brodie went on, "Anyway, I've got to bring Cready-Smythe out."

"What has he done for you?"

"He's in trouble."

"He got himself into it, so let him get out of it, himself."

"Shane, you know I've got to hang on."

"Then I stay, too," she said.

"I, too," Dr Huang chimed in. "I can not go back without Dr Sheng and Wang."

"Now, look, one of you must go back," he said. "I think it should be you, Dr Huang." He waved aside her protests. "You have seen what they are doing here and can tell your government, and they can take action to obtain the release of your two countrymen." She thought about this for a moment, then nodded her head.

"I go back," she said.

"Wali will go with you," Brodie said. He picked up two of the dead terns, handing one to Shane, the other to the Chinese doctor. "Have a look at these birds and see if there's anything strange about them—apart from the fact they've got the wrong plumage for the season."

At the back of the cave, in torchlight, they examined the three dead birds; all had been surgically doctored like the two ruffs they had caught, they had winter plumage and the migratory urge to set off for warmer quarters. For ten minutes they peered at the terns before Dr Huang spotted the curious fact. "But these birds are all the same," she cried.

"We know that—they're all Caspian terns," Brodie agreed.

"I do not mean this . . . I mean, they are like identical twins, unicellular twins."

She was right. On holding up the birds to compare them, they realized they were exact replicas of each other; every greyish streak on their head, the black patches round their eyes and every mark on their scarlet beaks corresponded. Stranger still, the brownish mottling on their wings might have been reproduced by some meticulous artist, it looked so much alike. Spreading their large wings, they matched them against each other. Not a millimetre difference.

"They've been bred from the same parents," Shane suggested.

Brodie shook his head. Again, he recalled that old Indian fisherman saying how these birds behaved as one, and this he had observed himself yesterday. "No," he said. "Even a clutch of eggs from one bird are different. There's something we've missed."

"Anyway, I can see what it means," Shane murmured. "If they're bred alike, they'll all follow the same migration route and return to the same breeding area."

Brodie nodded. Evidently, someone had worked out a whole strategy around these birds. And the others in the glass aviaries? What were they and what was happening to them? All these questions added up to another reason why he could not quit; with all his brains, Cready-Smythe did not have the technical equipment to understand what those labs were perpetrating down there.

Brodie broke off his reflections; he had to act. First, he briefed Wali and Dr Huang. Their safest route lay through the hills, backtracking to the tunnel under the frontier. They might have to risk covering some ground during the day when they had gone beyond the two lookout posts on the hills. They had four days' rations and they should also take one of the dead terns as evidence. If they left now, they would have one, perhaps two hours' start on their pursuers; if they survived the first day, they should succeed in crossing into Sinkiang. Everyone helped them pack and they slipped over the ridge to take the short-cut over the hill.

Brodie was breaking open the rucksacks left by the two Chinese and taking stock of the explosives they had carried. It was not dynamite, but a plastic explosive that looked like RDX (hexogen). They also had a Chinese machine-pistol like a Sten, and two revolvers. Shigo had turned out several lengths of quick and slow powder fuses and a dozen detonators that looked flimsy and rather dangerous. Sheng had also brought fifty yards of twin-flex which he could use to good effect. He gave Shigo the detonators and carried the plastic explosive himself as they groped their way to the rock overhang that lay to the right of their cave. Shane he had left to make them breakfast.

Brodie and Shigo set to work. They searched for small crevasses in the rock and, with brittle, dead fingers gouged them deeper with a sheath-knife and pen-knives. In half a dozen of these cracks, they buried some of the plastic explosive, priming it, leading several yards of fuse from it then tamping the holes with earth. Brodie varied the amount of plastic explosive and marked each charge carefully. It took just over an hour and a half to place all the charges, for they had to avoid making the slightest noise or dislodging the smallest stone that might have alerted the searchers below. For the last and biggest charge, he used one of the detonators with terminals to which he tied the ends of the twin-flex, then ran this down to the cave. There, while they ate breakfast, he explained to Shane how she could detonate the main charge by touching the two wires across two torch batteries. "What happens if I do that?" she asked.

"Let's hope you don't have to find out," he said. "But if you do touch those wires to the batteries, just keep your head down and stay in your cave."

XVIII

HE ORDERED SHIGO to bury the two dead terns under a pile of scree then went over the various moves the Hunza must make after Brodie gave himself up. If the worst happened to Cready-Smythe and himself, Shigo must take Shane south to Belkuz hamlet and hope someone would contact them; if not, somehow or other they must cross the Afghan frontier and get back into the Hunza Valley.

To Shane, he lied, saying he must draw the searchers off the hillside and would return when he had made the place safe. Quarter of an hour before dawn, he climbed the hill behind the waterfall then struck south along the ridge and descended a mile the other side of the camp on the west side. He saw the first patrols leave the camp, but made no attempt to hide; within ten minutes, they had spotted and pursued him; he turned and started to run up the hill, but when several shots whined past his head and spattered in the frozen earth round him, he dived for cover behind a parapet of rock. Before the patrol closed in, he emerged with his hands above his head. As the soldiers approached, he noted the green piping of the élite KGB border guards on their tunic; one of them wore a major's red tabs and stripes and had a mujik's squat, hulking build. Aiming his revolver at Brodie, he barked in Russian, "Who are you and what are you doing here?"

Brodie shook his head, replying in English that he did not understand. On the major's order, two troopers pinioned his arms while a third searched him for weapons but found nothing. They marched him along the lakeside and into the camp and down to the building he had taken for the military headquarters. Opening a door, they thrust him into an office. It had a plain wooden table, rough wooden chairs, a wardrobe, a filing cabinet and a clock that stood at six thirty-five—five minutes fast by his own watch. Dumped into a chair, he had his hands bound behind him.

Through the window to his left, he could observe a couple of dozen armed men scouring the hillside. How long before they reached the waterfall? A few minutes later, a door opened on his right and a tall man entered; on his unbuttoned tunic, Brodie spotted the stars of a KGB colonel; he had a smooth face, close-cropped blond hair and looked fortyish; in one hand, he carried a mug of tea, in the other an unlit cigarette. "Another spy," he grunted in Russian.

"Like the other one, he speaks only English, Colonel Krotkov," the major said in Russian.

"What is your name?" the colonel asked in guttural, accented English. While speaking, he crimped the cardboard tube of his papirosa, ran his lighter flame over the tobacco before putting the cigarette in his mouth and lighting it. His curious, bleached-blue eyes fixed on the scar-tissue patches on Brodie's face. "Your name?" he repeated.

"Dr Bolanz," Brodie replied. "You'll find my passport in my inside pocket."

At this, Colonel Krotkov and his major stared at each other before the major made his search. In a zipped anorak pocket he found the passport Brodie had taken from the man calling himself Dr Ernst Wolfgang Bolanz, passing it across the desk to the colonel. As he studied it, Brodie could see he was drawing the right conclusions; they had captured Bolanz and he had talked. "Where did you get this?" he said in a grating voice.

"It is my passport."

"You are lying," the colonel shouted, then flung an order at the major who gripped Brodie round the throat with both hands and squeezed. In the set of his bristly face and the light in those cruel, green eyes, Brodie saw this man would garotte him slowly without the slightest compunction. "The truth," he roared, squeezing harder. Blood was pulsing then hammering in Brodie's head and he felt the pressure distend his face and eyeballs. Suddenly Krotkov shouted to the major to stop. "Your name," he barked.

"I've told you—Bolanz, Ernst Wolfgang of 15 bis Hernalser Hauptstrasse, Vienna—near the railway bridge."

"What are you doing here?"

"I'm an Austrian doctor with the British and Chinese mountaineering expedition to Mustagh Ata," Brodie gasped.

"Why did you cross our frontier?"

"What frontier?"

"The frontier between the Soviet Union and the People's Republic of China."

"Sorry," Brodie murmured. "We must have missed it in the dark."

"How many were in your party?"

"Six altogether," Brodie lied.

"We have found four," Krotkov said. "Where are the other two?"

Brodie twisted his head to the left and nodded at the window and the mountain beyond. "Up there, waiting for you—one's under the waterfall and the other is further up the hill." Again, the colonel and major stared at each other and he could see them wondering why he had volunteered so much information. "But you'll never catch them," he said.

"Why do we not catch them?"

"I shall tell you later."

"Tell us now," Krotkov snarled and nodded to his major, who drew out and punched Brodie between the eyes, knocking his head back and stunning him. A big mujik fist buried itself in his stomach and, as his head snapped forward, the man caught him on the cheek with his bunched knuckles. Brodie felt his mouth fill with blood and he spat it all over the major's tunic and trousers. Those green eyes narrowed and the man came at him, his hands ready to fasten on his throat once more. "Wait," Brodie shouted.

"Yes?" the colonel prompted.

"Call off your performing bear and I'll answer your questions."

"Enough, Tikonov," the colonel said in Russian. "Now, those questions," he barked at Brodie.

"But they have to be the right questions."

"What do you mean, right questions?"

"Well, for instance, why have you only seventeen Caspian terns in your lakeside cage this morning? I can answer that. I trapped three of them last night and sent them over the hills." He smiled. "Of course, I put a few messages on their legs before I released them and they flew off."

Hearing this, the colonel now looked worried. "When did you do this?" he asked.

Brodie glanced at the clock which now registered ten to seven. "Five hours ago," he replied. "They'll either be well into Sinkiang or over Pakistan by now."

Banging his mug on the table and screwing out his cigarette, the colonel rose and left the office. Brodie could imagine him standing outside, counting the terns in their huge sea aviary. When he returned his face had gone white. "Idiot," he muttered, picking up the phone on his table and dialling an internal number. He apologized for the early hour, then explained in Russian what he had heard and verified from the spy he had caught this morning. From the one-sided discussion, Brodie concluded that the colonel was speaking to one of the scientists, who was evidently asking what had been written on the messages tied to the bird's legs. Putting down the phone the colonel snapped, "What did you write on those birds?"

"What one normally writes on a bird ring."

Now the colonel was shaking with fury; he marched round his desk and picked up the slim figure of Brodie, chair and all, shaking him until his teeth rattled and his head spun. "What did you write?"

"Put me down," Brodie said. When Krotkov complied, he said, "I gave the map reference of this camp where the birds had been released and told whoever caught them to report the fact to you—or to the Nature Protection Commission of the USSR Academy of Sciences."

"Anything else?"

"Oh yes, I forgot," Brodie murmured. "I said the birds had been purposely infected with a virus like shingles or chicken-pox."

"You wrote that," Colonel Krotkov muttered, and Brodie nodded. "Then you have just written a death certificate for yourself and your fellow-spies." He clenched his fist and brought it down on the crown of Brodie's head as though punching a nail into the floor; it jarred Brodie's spine from the brain bulb down to his tail.

"I wonder what the Chinese will do when they discover you have murdered two of their high-ranking officials," Brodie asked. His query earned him a blow on the face. Out of the corner of his eye, he was observing the armed platoon labouring up the mountain, each man searching the ground on both his flanks; in half an hour, they would reach the cave where Shane was hiding; she must be watching too, he thought, and wondering what to do and what had happened to him. As he reflected, he became aware the colonel and his major were marking time, waiting for someone or something; the colonel ordered himself another mug of tea with a fresh lemon slice and lit another papirosa. A door banged then their own door opened and two men stepped into the room. One of them was a tubby figure with a jowly face, pouched eyes and dark, receding hair. Brodie guessed he must be Nikolai Burov, the molecular biologist. Behind him came someone Brodie had no need to speculate about, for he had met the man before when he first encountered the bird disease. It was the man who called himself Josef Dettwiler.

Dettwiler was staring at him, his grey-green eyes narrowing. "But I met this man in a village just beyond the Afghan border in Pakistan," he said to the colonel. "What did you say your name was?"

"Bolanz . . . Ernst Wolfgang, of 15 bis . . ." He never completed his phrase, for Dettwiler smashed a fist into his face, toppling him and the chair. "You don't look like Bolanz," he said.

"Neither did Bolanz," Brodie got out, as he lay on the wooden floor.

Dettwiler kicked him in the ribs. "What has happened to Bolanz?" he snapped.

"He will be tried for spying with the five others," Brodie said. "If he confesses to everything, he might only get twenty years."

Two pairs of hands picked him and his chair off the floor and set him upright again. "So, you set a trap for Bolanz," Dettwiler said.

"And Sergeant Ivan Vasilevich Shirokov and the others with their false passports," Brodie replied. "They will all confess."

"That won't do you any good," Dettwiler shouted. "Where is the woman doctor who was with you when we first met?"

"I told him," Brodie said, nodding towards the KGB colonel. "Up on the hillside." He fixed his eyes on each of them in turn. "But if you touch one hair of her head, I shall destroy this camp and all of you with it."

Dettwiler and the two officers had a good laugh at this, but Burov did not even smile. Brodie faced Colonel Krotkov. "You had better call your men off, colonel, unless you want to lose quite a few of them." He looked at the clock which now registered two minutes to seven. "You have seven minutes to get them off the mountain," he said.

"He's bluffing," Dettwiler said. "It's like his Bolanz story."

"You'll know if I'm bluffing in six minutes thirty seconds," Brodie said, jerking his hand at the clock.

"What have you done?" It was the man he had taken for Professor Burov who spoke.

"Never mind—just tell Krotkov to get his men off the hillside."

Burov turned to the colonel and began speaking so rapidly in Russian that Brodie caught only half a dozen sentences; but in these he was urging Krotkov to call off his men or he would take responsibility for whatever happened. Abruptly, the colonel bellowed an order to Major Tikonov who ran from the office; they could see him sprint across to the camp entrance where he fired several revolver shots to attract the attention of his two platoons; he ran up the hillside, bawling at the men to return at the double to the camp. Brodie and the two scientists watched from the window as they raced and slithered downhill towards the camp.

Now, everyone in the small office had his eyes riveted on the clock hands, moving towards five past seven. Even Dettwiler's scepticism seemed to have dissolved and he, too, appeared tense as the second hand came up to record that last minute. But nothing happened. Everyone turned to stare at Brodie, who still looked at the clock, wondering whether Shigo had got the right time.

Dettwiler's grey-green eyes wrinkled into a grin. "I told you he was . . ."

At that second, they heard a dull report that reverberated down the valley, followed by a rumbling, clattering sound that sent shockwaves through their office. High above them, loosened by the blast, a pile of frozen scree and glacier ice had broken through the rock outcrop and had begun to slide down the sheer mountain face gathering momentum and more scree; out of this vast heap, large boulders were bouncing and racketing downwards towards the camp edge. Already alerted by Tikonov, the soldiers in the end huts had heard the detonation and spotted the landslide and were running full-out for safety towards the middle of the compound.

Dettwiler rounded on Brodie. "You must be crazy to do a thing like that."

"No crazier than you and your bosses who set up this place," Brodie came back.

"You could have killed those people," the scientist rapped, pointing to the half-dozen fleeing soldiers.

"And what are you trying to do with your contaminated birds?"

As they argued, the first rocks smashed down a section of the fence and flattened two wooden huts near the camp perimeter before plunging into the lake; a mass of smaller boulders and frozen earth followed in their wake, crushing the fence and engulfing the ruins of the huts. Brodie had not foreseen this, but the bulk of the avalanche halted fifty yards from the camp fence, blocked by a deep cleft in the hill and a rocky spur. Yet, poised dangerously, it needed only a nudge to set it in motion again. He observed how the KGB colonel, the two scientists and the KGB troopers had their eyes fixed not only on that loose slag but also on the huge pyramid of scree dammed behind the outcrop of igneous rock a mile above them. Both the KGB colonel and Dettwiler trained field glasses on the rocky ledge, obviously aware of the catastrophe they could face if that mass began to slip. Neither of them gave a sign of having spotted Shigo.

"If you try to find either of the people on that hill, they have orders to fire all the other charges," Brodie murmured. "And if I'm not released with the other three prisoners by this time tomorrow and given safe conduct to the frontier, those two people up there have orders to detonate all the explosive charges and destroy the camp."

"So, now you're playing poker," Dettwiler said.

"Yuri, shut your mouth," Burov snapped. To Brodie, he said, "You would not dare do that—in any case, you would be committing suicide."

"I have my orders."

"Orders! From whom?"

"From one of the men you captured last night."

"The Englishman?" Brodie nodded and Burov went on, "He will counter that instruction, I know."

"Never."

"I shall ask him."

Brodie shook his head. "Any order he gives has to come to me direct—and without any of your mujik majors persuading him."

"He will write this order to you."

Brodie shook his head. Burov thought for several minutes before turning to the KGB colonel. Speaking in his rapid Russian, he stressed they must at all costs save the camp and the birds; they could not afford to see years of work eradicated by a madman who looked as though he would carry out this second threat; therefore, they should allow him to consult his superior who seemed a much more amenable person; it would do no harm since they could not escape, and it would allow them to buy time so that they could capture the two people on the mountain and defuse those explosive charges. Moscow would never forgive them if they allowed a homicidal and suicidal individual to set back strategic scientific programmes that had taken years to plan and put into operation; none of those responsible for such a disaster would survive. Brodie perceived that the colonel had already reached much the same conclusions without having to listen to Burov's advocacy. His KGB bosses would make short work of one of their officers who had been humiliated by a terrorist with a few bits of explosive. He would finish his days either digging salt or developing some remote part of the Siberian tundra with other labour-camp inmates. "I suppose we must play for time," he muttered finally. "Tikonov, search the prisoner and take him to the guard-house with the others."

Brodie found his hands freed. Tikonov stripped off his anorak and turned its pockets inside out, then searched his shirt and trouser pockets. They yielded nothing. Binding Brodie's hands in front, he dug a revolver into his back and pushed him through the door, following with two guards. Brodie hoped Shane would be watching them through her field-glasses and know that he was still alive, and that his threat had succeeded so far. As he had assumed, the guard-house sat in the centre of the compound, not far above the laboratories and behind the admin building. Passing one of the glass-domed houses, he caught the fetid whiff of caged birds and their droppings from an air-conditioner. At the guard-house, a soldier flung open the main door and led them along a corridor to a door at which stood two more KGB guards. Opening this door, they shoved Brodie inside, then banged the door behind him and locked it.

XIX

CREADY-SMYTHE LAY ON one of the two iron beds under a Russian army blanket. They had obviously tortured him; red and blue bruises had puffed out his oblong face and his eyes had shrunk into the mass of swollen and painful flesh around them; they had ripped his thick shirt and his exposed chest had caked with blood that had dripped from his face and nose. On hearing the door bang, he rotated his head slowly as though it hurt, then peered for several seconds at Brodie before his mind grasped who he was. "So they got you too, Paul," he croaked.

Brodie pointed a finger at his ear, indicating they had probably bugged the room. Placing his mouth against Cready-Smythe's ear, he briefed him on what he had done, why they had stopped hunting for Shane and Shigo and had allowed them to meet in this room. "You're a fool," Cready-Smythe whispered. "You should have made for the frontier when we didn't come back."

"They'd have caught us, and we wouldn't have had the chance to blackmail them," Brodie whispered. He looked at the man on the other bed. Had Cready-Smythe not whispered the name, Sheng, he would never have recognized him; his mandarin face seemed a mass of bruised flesh and dried blood. Cready-Smythe murmured that Wang was lying in the camp clinic with a bullet in his hip and another in his right shoulder. He lifted himself up on one elbow. "Ask them for some water," he said.

Brodie went and banged on the door. When a guard opened it, he signed he wanted water; he heard them arguing among themselves, then one clumped off, to return five minutes later with a pitcher of water and a tin mug. Brodie forced some past Sheng's thickened lips then wet part of his torn tunic and cleaned his face and head. Cready-Smythe drank half a mug of water, then cleaned up his face. "Pretty rough, these tartars," he said through swollen lips.

"Who tortured you?"

"A big, blond, birdwatching type."

"Dettwiler."

"The man you met. There was another character, a mujik with gold teeth."

"Tikonov."

Leaning on Brodie's shoulder, Cready-Smythe hobbled to the one small window which had two guards outside; it had a restricted view on the admin building and part of the sea-bird cage and the lake beyond; they could also see part of one lab and a bird-house. "What are they really doing with these birds?" Cready-Smythe asked.

"We've got some idea," Brodie said, explaining how he had snared three terns that looked exactly alike and had been doctored in the same way as the ruffs; he had sent one tern over the hills with Dr Huang and Wali, burying the others.

"Birds are no good without the scientific records," the SIS man whispered. "Somehow, we must get in there and grab as many files as we can."

"Then what—run like hell over the roof of the world?" Brodie said, bitingly.

Cready-Smythe clapped Brodie on the shoulder. "You'll hit on a way, Paul," he said. "That's what you came in to do."

For the rest of the morning, no-one bothered them, though Brodie got them to open the back window when their small room became choking hot. At midday, the guards brought in a tray containing three bowls of soup and a hunk of bread. Brodie fed Sheng who scarcely had the energy to swallow the gruel and breadcrumbs. "I used to think Brown Windsor was the world's worst soup," Cready-Smythe grumbled, forcing the thin mixture down. While they ate, he whispered what he had learned about the guard-house and camp routine. It seemed the lab staff and soldiers used the canteen at the same time, midday and seven at night. New guards took over at eight o'clock and went off duty at six in the morning. After they had tortured and flung him into this room, Cready-Smythe had lain and listened to the birds in the domed houses and on the lake; they all appeared restless and sleepless. Brodie listened, wondering how they could take advantage of all these facts. "We haven't much time," he murmured.

"What do you mean?"

Cupping a hand over Cready-Smythe's ear, he explained how he and Shigo had planted Sheng's plastic explosive all round the spur holding back a mountain of scree, how Shigo had fired one charge that morning and would detonate the others at seven o'clock next morning unless someone caught him or he, Brodie, countermanded the order. Shane, too, had orders to destroy the camp if they tried to take her prisoner.

"So, that's why they're leaving us alone," Cready-Smythe said.

"They're probably trying to figure out a way to trap them."

"In either event, we haven't got much chance."

A guard threw open the door, and another man watched with his Kalashnikov machine-pistol at his hip as a third guard entered with three mugs of tea without milk, sugar or lemon. He took the tray and soup bowls away. When the man returned to collect their tea mugs, Brodie pointed to himself and Cready-Smythe. "Toilet," he said. One at a time, they were escorted by two guards to the latrine at the end of the guard-house. There, by standing on the chemical toilet, Brodie could glimpse the hill behind. They were still searching and half a dozen men had reached a point halfway up the hill towards the waterfall. Shane would be watching them with those batteries in her hand, ready to touch the wires to the contacts. Would she have the courage? Shigo would have vanished round the back of the hill while they searched. Brodie sited the canteen with its brace of propane cylinders, and the generator house. Cready-Smythe brought back an intriguing piece of information from his visit to the toilets; they used the canteen as a cinema and, at nine o'clock, they were showing *Miners of the Donbas*, followed by the Red Army Choir. "A hilarious evening," he commented.

"I suppose they've got to show them how lucky they are down on the bird farm."

Just after seven Tikonov appeared, beckoned with a hooked finger at Brodie and marched him, under escort, to headquarters and the colonel's office. As he entered, he broke stride and cursed. They had seized Shane. "Paul . . . thank God, you're alive," she called from the chair to which they had tied her. She gave a sigh, then turned to face Krotkov. "That was a dirty lie your men told me," she said, bitterly. To Brodie, she said, "They shouted you were dying and had begged to see me." She shrugged. "Anyway, I couldn't have done what you wanted me to do."

"Where is S?" he asked.

"He's all right."

"Shut up, both of you," Tikonov roared. "No talking." He emphasized the order by drawing the back of his hand across Brodie's face.

"Don't do that," Shane cried. For that, he slapped her with the flat of his hand.

Burov and the man they knew as Dettwiler came into the office, the latter smiling when he caught sight of Shane. "Ah, the good doctor from Runghar," he said, then turned to Brodie. "You are running out of arguments for your survival, aren't you, Dr Bolanz."

"We discovered where they placed the explosives," Colonel Krotkov remarked. "We have defused the charges."

"Good work, colonel," Burov commented.

"There is one more thing," Krotkov continued, and barked an instruction to Tikonov who left the room to return shortly with two soldiers carrying the slack, soiled bodies of two Caspian terns. "Our dogs found these buried near the waterfall," the colonel said.

"There were three missing," Burov said. "Where's the third one?" he asked Brodie.

"In China, I hope."

"Answer the professor's question," Tikonov bellowed, ramming his big fist into Brodie stomach, which caused him to double up.

"Stop that, you brute," Shane cried.

"It'll be your turn next," Tikonov growled, but his colonel motioned him to shut his mouth.

"What did you do with the other bird?" Burov insisted.

"I released it as soon as I had trapped it, and tied a message to its leg."

"He's lying," Dettwiler rapped out.

"We'll soon find out," Tikonov snapped. "He'll get a dose of what the others have had." Gripping Brodie's arm, he twisted it, sadistically, behind his back and applied pressure. "Tell them the truth," he shouted.

Brodie twisted to take some of the pressure off his arm; he lifted his foot and brought it down with everything he had on the Russian's boot. With a yell that filled the small office, the major hopped on one foot, releasing his hold. His men grabbed hold of Brodie who was tensing, expecting a blow from a rifle-butt when suddenly a bang echoed through the camp followed by that slight quivering underfoot they had experienced earlier that day. Everyone except the guards rushed out to gaze upwards; several soldiers who had been searching the hillside were fleeing before the landslide, which was following the same track as the previous one. Through the window, Brodie and Shane observed two soldiers disappear under the tumbling mass of rock and sludge which was heading for the east end of the camp. "Shigo, you marvel," Brodie called to Shane as they watched the avalanche pick up the pile of debris left that morning and thunder towards the camp edge. It swept away part of the fence repaired a few hours earlier and fifty more yards; it crushed two barracks buildings, sliced away part of a lab and carried two mangled trucks and a jeep with it on the way to the lake. No-one knew how many men had been in the barrack-rooms or the lab section. Everyone in the camp stood stunned by the abrupt and unexpected disaster. For minutes after the avalanche had stopped, the ground kept vibrating with its impact; now, the top end of the camp was sealed by a wall of slag and frozen mud fully twenty feet high. Brodie heard the colonel issue orders. He instructed someone to call the roll; he berated Tikonov for failing to unearth all the explosives on the mountain as well as allowing the sixth man to go uncaptured; he issued directions about rebuilding the fence and clearing part of the ground to search for victims under the destroyed barrack-rooms and lab. When he returned to his office with Burov and Dettwiler, all three looked ashen-faced, and Brodie could imagine what was passing through their minds. If another explosive charge set the rest of that scree moving, there would be nothing left either of them or their camp. Dettwiler, especially, was gazing, grim-faced, at Brodie as though he could not credit anyone with perpetrating such crazy acts.

Colonel Krotkov had gone purple with rage. He rounded on Brodie. "You will order that man to come down the hill now," he roared. "Either that or we shoot you all, one by one, as spies."

"Just touch one of us, and the man up there will bring the whole mountain down and destroy you and your camp," Brodie came back. "If you do not release us by seven o'clock, he will do that anyway." Looking at Burov and Dettwiler, he continued, "The only things that might survive are the birds and they'll fly east and south and give your little horror games away."

"Order up several helicopters and they'll find him, colonel," Dettwiler suggested.

"And have him blow the whole hillside down around us," Krotkov snarled. He thumbed at Brodie. "He won't let his mad accomplice carry out his threat while his beloved companion is here, will he?"

"What's the difference between being shot or buried?" Shane put in.

Krotkov scowled at her. "You're all mad," he growled. He turned to Brodie. "What brought you here, anyway?"

"We came to see what you were doing, and when we've done that we'll go."

"They can't be serious," Dettwiler said. He then addressed Krotkov. "You can't allow them to make conditions, colonel."

"Of course not," Krotkov agreed. "I have no intention of surrendering to blackmail." He twisted the hollow cardboard tube of his papirosa between his thumb and forefinger, stuck it in his mouth and lit it. He pointed a finger at Brodie. "I give you until six o'clock tomorrow to call off your man."

"And if I don't . . . ?"

"I shall start by shooting your fellow-spy, the Englishman, then the Chinese, then this woman, then yourself."

"And if I do . . . ?"

"You will be flown to Moscow and placed on trial as spies. You will be given a fair trial and I can promise you will not be tortured."

Brodie reflected for several moments before replying. "I shall have to discuss all this with the Englishman," he said.

"Accorded."

"If he agrees, I shall have to contact my man by climbing the mountain to where he may be hiding."

"It's a trap, colonel," Dettwiler warned.

"What else can we do?" Burov asked.

"Nothing," the colonel retorted. "We have too many hostages and if he tries to play games, we shoot his friends and his companion here—and they'll be picked up between here and the frontier."

"I have one more request," Brodie said. "This lady should be allowed to share our room."

"That makes guarding you all the easier," Colonel Krotkov said, and ordered the sentries to escort Brodie and Shane to the guardhouse. On the way, Brodie saw the KGB colonel and the scientific staff were taking his threat seriously; three trucks stood outside the labs and admin buildings and the civilian workers were loading boxes into them, evidently ensuring the camp records did not vanish under any avalanche. If he guessed right, those boxes contained the sort of data that he and Cready-Smythe had come to collect.

He noted, too, they had cancelled the cinema performance, and from the activity in the labs and the barrack area, he inferred the whole camp was on the alert or stand-by. Back in their room, he whispered what had happened to Cready-Smythe. "But they'll follow you up that hill, or post snipers and pick you off," he protested. "If they catch or kill Shigo, we're finished."

"I know," Brodie said. "But he may go ahead and bury us all under an avalanche—so I've got to stop him and play for time."

Shane did what she could for Sheng. After examining him, she said they had probably broken a rib and might have caused some kidney damage when they beat him up. She demanded and got surgical tape to strap his ribs, and morphine for his pain. When their soup and bread arrived that evening, she sent it back, peremptorily, saying they would only eat decent food. To their astonishment, the guards returned with four bowls of bortsch soup, then tinned stew, potatoes and beans; they also had sweet biscuits with their mugs of tea, and even sugar. When they had eaten, Cready-Smythe, Shane and Brodie put their heads together to pool what information they had about the camp layout—the location of the armoury, the generator house, the clinic where Wang was being treated, the bird-houses, the labs and admin. Shane made up two beds on the floor for Cready-Smythe and Brodie, she and Sheng taking the bedsteads.

Just before light-out, Krotkov pushed open the door and called to Brodie. "What is your decision?"

"I shall go and tell my man to surrender himself and his explosives," Brodie replied.

XX

JUST BEFORE DAWN, a guard rapped on the door, Brodie pulled on his anorak and boots and followed two soldiers to headquarters where the colonel was waiting. "If you have me followed, or try to capture or shoot my friend, I cannot prevent him from destroying your camp," he told Krotkov, who nodded. Brodie left by the main gate, but he did not climb the mountain face, choosing to make a long, right-handed detour and ascend along the ridge which capped the waterfall to the pile of scree. Shigo would spot him and reason what he was doing to keep the troops well away from his usual hiding-place and make sure they were unsighted from the mountain top lookout posts. Brodie felt certain the colonel and his tame bear, Tikonov, had deployed men on either flank to watch their movements; he went gently, halting every quarter of an hour to allow Shigo the time and opportunity to pick a safe place.

As he reached the summit of the spur, a pebble rattled off the rocks near his feet; it had come from a sharp peak nearly a thousand feet above him. Peering into the morning twilight, he discerned the spot Shigo had chosen—a small cave on the sheer face of a splintered peak. No-one could possibly climb that pinnacle and surprise him from the rear, and his view dominated the whole valley, although he remained hidden from the camp and the lookout posts. Brodie started scrambling upwards through loose moraine and over the ground, frozen in the last few hours. He had arrived to within three hundred feet of Shigo's cave when he heard the Hunza call. "Paul-sahib—to the right." Brodie glanced in that direction. Just below him and behind a pile of rocks two of Tikonov's platoon were setting up the mortar they must have carried up the hill during darkness. In a few minutes they would be lobbing bombs at Shigo's cave; and if he made a dash for it by the only exit Brodie could see, he would expose himself to fire from Tikonov's snipers.

Brodie did not stop to consider his own danger, but cursed himself for leading Shigo into a trap through his own stupidity. On all fours he clambered upward, covering the rocky section between him and the cave in ten minutes to flop, gasping behind the rocks around the entrance. Shigo dragged him inside. He wore that grin nothing seemed to efface. "You have seen Shane?" he asked.

"Shane's okay. Smythe-sahib is fit enough to travel, but the Chinese are both sick." Brodie thumbed over his shoulder. "How deep is this cave?"

"Twenty feet—deep enough for fighting."

Still on his belly, Brodie inched further into the cave then stood up and began to explore it; here, they would have protection against any number of mortar bombs fired from that downhill position with their high trajectory. Shigo whispered he had found the place twenty-four hours before and had brought the machine-pistol and two revolvers the Chinese had left behind with some rations. Those weapons would account for quite a few of the KGB company if they made a frontal attack. Brodie's only doubt: How did they get out? There appeared only one way—straight downhill through Tikonov's platoon. And after dark anybody might creep up and lob grenades into this narrow cave. Shigo was watching his face. "There is way round mountain," he murmured.

"For you, maybe," Brodie grunted. "But I could never climb that peak and get round that mountain even in broad daylight."

"I came thus," Shigo said and was drawing a diagram on the cave floor to explain when they had to throw themselves on the ground as the first mortar bomb exploded above the cave, showering the entrance with rock splinters. Seconds later, another bomb landed just below the cave, deafening them with its detonation and forcing them to cover their heads with their hands as metal and rock shrapnel ricocheted off the cave mouth. For half an hour they had to retreat to the back of the cave and erect a small parapet of stones to shelter them from the bombs that now fell every few seconds around the entrance.

However, the Russians had not reckoned that they might trigger off small landslides in these dangerous mountains. Their salvos of mortar bombs loosened the rocks and scree heaped at the base of the pinnacle and started a small avalanche which came so close to the mortar position the crew had to scatter out of its path. Things grew too risky for them when an unexploded mortar bomb rattled downhill and came to rest ten yards from their mortar position. They decided to move, but as they exposed themselves, Shigo wounded one man in the side, firing single shots with the machine-pistol. Before they could pull out, he and Brodie started a small landslide of their own which swept away the mortar, twisted its barrel and forced the crew to abandon their cover.

For half an hour nothing stirred, then Major Tikonov bustled up the hill to within fifty yards of their cave, his square face puffing and livid with the effort. Shigo placed two shots within a foot of the KGB major compelling him to dive behind a small pile of rocks and stay there. "Throw down your arms and come out with your hands raised," he bellowed.

"Just make one move and we'll put several bullets in you," Brodie shouted back, pointing up the threat by sending a shot whanging off the rocks above Tikonov's head.

"We shall starve you out."

"We have food and water for a week," Brodie called. "You'll be pretty thirsty by sunset."

"The colonel promises to spare your lives if you surrender."

"Tell him to stuff that with all his other broken promises."

They took turns to watch Tikonov and the other men on the hillside as well as the camp. Nobody moved, perhaps because the platoon feared for the safety of their commander, lying broiling in the sun within easy range of any marksman. At midday, Shigo brewed them tea; he even produced flour to make four thin chupattis and opened a tin of ham and another of processed cheese on which they lunched. Brodie had exaggerated by declaring they had food for a week; at most, they might withstand two days of siege. But in any case, they had to move after dark to try to rescue the others.

"How much explosive have we left?" he asked and Shigo produced just over two pounds of plastic explosive and twenty metres of quick fuse. "Russians took all the rest," he complained. So, they had a Chinese nine-millimetre machine-pistol with about a hundred rounds of ammunition, two revolvers with the same number of bullets and plastic dynamite the size of a small loaf. Enough to do some damage, Brodie thought.

They sat out the rest of that day. Below them, the platoon still did not stir; nor did Tikonov, who seemed scared to move an inch and lay pinned behind his shallow parapet suffering the slow, agonizing torture of thirst. While they kept vigil, Brodie briefed Shigo about the camp layout and went over the plan he had evolved during those waiting hours; but it meant they had to escape from their present trap and somehow penetrate the camp without being surprised. Brodie glanced at the pinnacle, a needle of sheer rock soaring above them. He was banking on the fact that neither Tikonov nor the KGB colonel would ever imagine anybody making that climb and traverse in dead darkness. He could hardly envisage it himself, even after Shigo had explained how he had done it in the opposite direction twice before.

Half an hour after sunset, they caught the sounds of several men creeping up the slope, and prepared for an attack; however, they were merely collecting their exhausted commander. It gave Brodie and Shigo a chance which they seized. Shouldering their rucksacks, they flitted out of the cave, feeling their way step by step towards the pinnacle. Without the Hunza man, Brodie would never have dared attempt that peak even in daylight. Fifty yards above the cave, it rose almost perpendicular, and they had to watch neither to make a noise nor dislodge stones that would warn the KGB platoon below them. Shigo began by roping them together, looping the rope around himself to give Brodie more confidence and support. He led the way, seeking and touch-testing footholds and handholds in the smooth and slippery mountain face, even placing Brodie's hands in crevices and projections. Their rope he kept taut by belaying it over rock spurs above their head.

Ten minutes after they started, Brodie's numb fingers missed a handhold, his feet slipped and he slithered five yards down into the darkness to dangle to and fro across the peak face, searching desperately for another hold. "Paul-sahib," Shigo whispered. "Push with your feet and I pull." Brodie managed to stop his pendulum motion and found a crevice for one foot. As he pushed upwards, Shigo tightened the rope over its belaying point and, inch by inch, he pulled Brodie upwards until he was able to grasp a rock and hang on. For minutes, they both stood motionless, Brodie hearing only his heartbeat and the blood pulsing in his ears. Another slip like that and he would have no nerves left.

Shigo was moving again, clawing upwards. A hundred feet above them, a ledge ran across the peak face. When they reached this, Brodie had to beg him to rest for quarter of an hour before he felt strong enough to tackle it. Along this eighteen-inch step, flattened against the rock face arms outstretched to feel for holds and balance themselves, they shuffled an inch at a time for half an hour that felt like eternity. Brodie followed blindly, scared to look at anything but the vague outline of Shigo to his right, feeling nothing but the rope pressure urging him sideways.

"Now, we go down, Paul-sahib," the Hunza whispered. That sounded easier, but they had turned the corner on to the worst face of the peak and had few handholds. Shigo reversed them, taking the rope strain while Brodie led and groped downwards a foot at a time, hearing and obeying the Hunza's whispered advice. He could not believe it when suddenly he sensed a slope under his feet rather than a sheer wall. Shigo dropped beside him on his haunches. "We done it," he whispered. Brodie sat down, his legs shaky; he fumbled in the knapsack to surface with Cready-Smythe's whisky and took a small gulp. Shigo, too. For the first time Brodie realized how cold it was on that mountain. "We go one mile and one half-mile that way," Shigo said, pointing north.

They still had to move cautiously in case Krotkov had put out patrols. Shigo led the way, with Brodie keeping his shadow in sight and covering him with a revolver. But they met nobody, probably because the colonel and Tikonov believed they were still in the cave and were therefore keeping surveillance on that part of the hill. As they descended the slope, approaching the eastern edge of the camp, Brodie caught Shigo by the arm to whisper, "The guards and the dogs." He gestured that they must go round by the lake. Ducking behind the ridge separating the two lakes, they reached the spot where they had hidden and watched the capture of Cready-Smythe and the Chinese. They shivered in the freezing wind as they both stripped naked then wrapped their clothing, firearms and munitions inside their groundsheets. They tucked this waterproof bundle into their rucksacks, then tied each other's rucksack straps round their backs to keep them under their chests and underwater as they swam.

Brodie slipped into the icy water which seemed to penetrate to his marrow. With Shigo a yard or two behind him, he made for the laboratories and the scientists' living quarters on the west side of the great aviary over the lake. Not a single tern moved as they swam close to the boom. When they touched bottom, they crept under the lee of the darkened laboratory. There, they dressed, tested their three weapons and filled their pockets with ammunition. Their rucksacks they hid in the space under one of the labs.

"Good luck, Shigo," Brodie said.

"Good luck, Paul-sahib."

In the camp, only one thing stirred—the canteen. To show how confident he felt, the colonel had permitted the showing of *Miners of the Donbas* and the Red Army Choir. Both men knew exactly what they had to do. Brodie led, wriggling on his stomach across the ground between the lab and the guard-house. At the rear window, both Russian soldiers were stamping up and down to keep the cold out of their bones; their cigarettes flowered in the dark. For several minutes, Brodie and Shigo timed their ten-pace patrol from one end of the building to the other. Splitting up, one went left and the other inched towards the right end. As the Russians about-turned and started back, Brodie and Shigo rose and brought their revolver butts down on their heads, felling them. Quickly, they stripped off the Russian uniforms, bound and gagged the men with their own clothing and lanyards and pushed them under the wooden building. Brodie stood on Shigo's shoulders and tapped on the window. Cready-Smythe edged it open and pulled him through. Brodie handed the SIS man the spare revolver and ammunition, then took the two uniforms from the Hunza; one he donned himself, the other he gave to Cready-Smythe, whose arms and legs protruded through the short tunic and trousers, giving him a scarecrow look. Sheng still looked weak, but game. They whispered to him that he must get to the clinic where Wang was held and rescue him when the chance came.

One by one, they dropped to the ground, Sheng first, then Shane followed by the two men. Brodie briefed everyone about his plan. *Miners of the Donbas* and the Red Army Choir would run for another forty-five minutes, he reckoned, and they must make every minute count. Cready-Smythe and Shigo would take care of the diesel tank and the propane cylinders; they would also put the radio operator and his transmitter out of commission. "Won't that alert somebody at the other end?" Shane asked.

"No—reception in these mountains is too dicey for them to notice," Cready-Smythe replied. Equipped with their share of munitions, plastic explosive, detonators and quick fuse, the SIS man and the Hunza crawled off.

Brodie tried to persuade Shane to stay, hidden, behind the labs, but she refused to be separated from him. They flitted through the camp, keeping to the shadow of the buildings until they reached the transport compound. Shane watched the sentinels on the perimeter fence and the two remaining dog-handlers while Brodie searched the five trucks, finally discovering the one in which they had placed the camp records. That, and the colonel's jeep he left alone; all the others he put out of action. To grab distributor heads meant raising the bonnets and risking exposure, so he simply drove his knife-blade through the tyres and ripped away the brake-fluid tubes from one of the front wheels. "Paul, darling—somebody's coming." Shane whispered.

Brodie pulled her under a truck and stood up himself. A torch beam fell on him and his ill-fitting uniform. "Lost something, comrade?" a voice said.

"Da," Brodie replied, stepping out of the torchlight. As the man advanced, Brodie chopped at his neck with the heel of his hand, then for good measure hit him over the head with his gun-butt. "Gag him," he whispered, and Shane pushed her handkerchief into the man's mouth before they bound him and thrust him under a truck. He used some of his ration of plastic explosive to mine the petrol dump beside the vehicle depot before they headed for the generator house.

There, they ran into snags. It took valuable time to locate the buried coaxial cables running from the dynamo and put a collar of plastic explosive round them, then fix a detonator and ten feet of quick fuse. Brodie had to work by feel, then bury his fuse and mark the spot. While he toiled with frozen fingers, Shane was gazing at the bird-houses. Light filtered through the seams of their wooden structure and glass domes; a twittering and a clatter of wings reached them. "Those poor birds," Shane murmured.

"I know," Brodie said. "It's sad."

Cready-Smythe and Shigo were waiting for them behind the lab, having done their job with the plastic explosive. "The KGB colonel's in his quarters," the SIS man whispered.

"And Burov and Dettwiler?"

"Burov's in the central lab, working. Dettwiler's in his hut."

From the makeshift cinema, they caught the strains of *Black Eyes* from the Red Army Choir which told them they had perhaps no more than quarter of an hour before three-quarters of the KGB company and most of the research staff emerged from the canteen. "Give us ten minutes then you grab the colonel," Brodie whispered. "Shigo, you contact the Chinaman and say he must rescue Wang when he hears the first bang. Then you take Dettwiler, the man from Runghar."

"Where are you going?" Cready-Smythe asked.

"To get your most important hostage—Burov."

XXI

A FEW STEPS took Brodie and Shane to the main lab. An entrance light burned and the door lay unlocked. Under a corridor door, they spotted another light. Brodie edged the door open. Burov sat, hunched over a bench, his eyes pressed against a binocular microscope. Only when Brodie walked over and pulled down the window blind did the scientist raise his head. For several seconds, he stared at Brodie in his ill-fitting KGB uniform before recognizing him. Brodie switched off the ultra-high-speed centrifuge and closed the tap of a Bunsen burner flaring under a retort. "Your experiments are finished for tonight, professor," he murmured.

Burov looked at the revolver in Brodie's hand, then at Shane. "How . . ." he stuttered.

"We haven't time to tell you."

They took stock of the lab. It had everything: the latest microscopes and micro-manipulators, a freeze-dryer and deep freezers for storing viruses and other microbes, several centrifuges of American and Japanese design, serried rows of test-tubes, jars of chemicals, bottles of serum and various vaccines. In one hatcher a dozen eggs were incubating, bantam-sized, grey-green eggs with a speckling of black, brown and grey. Caspian tern eggs. A second hatcher contained smaller eggs which he took for ruffs' with their milky hue and sepia mottling. A third hatcher was full of still smaller eggs which from their cream colour blotched and speckled with grey, orange and brown, they assumed were swallows'.

Brodie took one of the tern eggs and held it against the light. Through its mottled shell, he could discern the embryonic form of the chick. "Another twelve identical birds, professor," he murmured. Burov's face flushed and he assumed a guilty look. "What have you given these?" Brodie went on. "Bubonic plague, smallpox, cholera, a new form of polio, anthrax or just old-fashioned shingles?"

Burov did not answer. Brodie's eyes went to the wall charts and diagrams, the chemical formulae; all of them had the same theme, how to combine the two viruses of herpes zoster (shingles) and adenovirus Type 3 with a microbe called escherichia coli, a normal and benign inhabitant of the intestine in man and animals. Both Brodie and Shane could infer from these formulae that Burov had succeeded, by genetic manipulation, in building both viruses into the escherichia bacterium so that the bird droppings had become highly infectious, something they had proved, clinically, for themselves in the northern villages.

Shane went over to study more closely the various steps in the gene-splicing techniques Burov and Dettwiler had used; she cast an eye over the small library of text-books and specialist journals on microbiology and molecular biology in Russian and English. "You learned a lot at Cambridge, professor," she murmured.

"How did you know I was there?"

"You worked under Professor Kingslake, the man who wrote this book on molecular biology and inscribed this copy to you." She held up the book, and Burov nodded. She went on, "That was before I became his assistant, then his wife and his widow."

"Forgive me . . . I didn't know," Burov stammered.

While Shane and Burov were speaking, Brodie's eye ranged round the lab before it lighted on one of the files the Russian professor had been studying at his workbench. There, in Cyrillic script, presumably in Burov's own hand, were two words that pulled him up with a jerk. PROJECT ICARUS. So both Burov and Cready-Smythe had hit on the same code-word, one for the project and the other to destroy it. Whoever believed that coincidence of minds would believe anything! He turned to Burov.

"Shane's late husband taught you your genetics and microbiology—but he never thought you would use it to make biological weapons, and he never would have taught you to clone birds, would he?"

"They forced me."

"Always THEY," Brodie snapped back.

Suddenly, from the direction of the guard-house, someone bellowed a Russian oath, then a whistle blew, long, piercing blasts. Peering round the blind, Brodie saw half a dozen figures emerging at the double from the guard-house. They had finally discovered the empty room. "Shane, keep this on Burov and make for the truck," he said, handing her the revolver. He sprinted out of the lab and across to the generator-house; several soldiers were already on the move, but they ignored him, mistaking him for one of their own in his uniform. Brodie located the buried fuse end, applied a match to it and flattened himself against the generator building, counting five as the flame streaked towards the explosive. A flash and a bang no louder than a shotgun, but the detonation split the main coaxial cable apart. Immediately every light in the camp went out.

In the dead darkness, someone collided with him. It was Shigo. "Smythe-sahib has the big man and the colonel. They will wait outside the camp. I come for the bangs." Quickly, he showed Brodie where they had mined and fused the diesel tank, then lit the fuse. "How much did you use?"

"To make a big hole."

From the blast, he had used more than that. Even behind the generator building they got drenched in the acrid-tasting and foul-smelling gas-oil that spouted and sprayed from the tank when the explosion ripped it apart. Oil gushed from the tank, flowing through the camp and down the slope towards the lake.

"Where's the propane fuse?" Brodie asked.

Shigo pulled him to the right, behind the canteen from which most of the KGB company was now spilling, tripping over one another and cursing in the darkness. Finding the short fuse, Shigo lit it then grabbed Brodie. "This time, better run," he said. Run they did, putting fifty yards between themselves and the big propane tanks, then throwing themselves flat. But still they felt the blast of searing air go over their heads and the explosion shake the ground and resonate and reverberate down the valley and up the mountain. Burning liquid propane was gouting from the two vast steel bottles; against the flames, soldiers were scattering and yelling in fear; some who had been sprayed by propane were blazing like torches and running for the lake to plunge into the water. Several buildings had caught fire and from the canteen dozens of tins were exploding and burning fat and butter were tinting the flames green and orange.

By now, the propane had ignited the diesel oil and the flames were reaching the guard-house, the bird-houses and labs on their way to the lake. So transfixed were Brodie and Shigo by the sight of the blazing camp, they almost forgot their own danger. Above the din from men fleeing in every direction, they heard the twittering then the screeching of birds trapped in their closed, wooden aviaries. One by one, the three houses were gripped by the flames and destroyed within minutes; two of the glass domes erupted in a shower of glass and an odour of scorching flesh and feathers. No bird had survived. Brodie ran round the generator building to watch the burning propane and diesel oil spread over the water and under the vast aviary. Terrified by the flames and the heat, the seventeen terns were battering against the wire mesh in vain efforts to escape the flames. But none survived. Like petrol-soaked rags, they blazed for a few seconds before plunging into the burning pool, their raucous cries piercing the din as they died. Brodie turned away from this pitiful sight. They still had work to do, and he knew that Tikonov and his men would have witnessed the destruction of their camp and would be running down the mountain and at the camp gate within half an hour.

"Shigo, go and find Sheng and help him get his friend to the truck," he ordered.

Brodie had one more fuse to light and darted across to the transport area where he found the short fuse leading to the petrol drums and lit it. It gave him five seconds to reach the main entrance and he sprinted, head-down, away from the petrol dump. He had counted on this last explosion to cover their tracks, and it did. As the plastic explosive detonated, dozens of petrol drums shot into the air, then seemed to lift even higher on the pillar of fire that climbed into the night sky. Those soldiers within fifty yards ran for cover or headed for the lake as petrol rained and splashed on them; a thick ribbon of flame seemed to pursue them as the petrol sped towards the lake.

Brodie heard a shout from Shane and saw the colonel's jeep and their truck lying twenty yards beyond the main gate on the track leading west. When he got there, he saw Burov and Krotkov in the jeep with his old boss. Clever Cready-Smythe. He had forced the colonel to wear his full uniform and sat him in the front passenger seat to make it appear he was commanding this small detachment. Shane was sitting in the truck cabin with Dettwiler. Cready-Smythe had studied the map and waited long enough to give Brodie a rendezvous several miles down the track before digging Burov in the back and ordering him to drive off.

With the truck, they waited five long minutes before Shigo and the two Chinamen appeared. Brodie lost no time sending the two-ton vehicle bumping over the rough track on full headlights. At the most, they probably had two to four hours' start on their pursuit; for that fire was lighting the sky over miles and soon the nearest Russian border post or military unit would want to know what happened and why the camp had gone silent, or lost radio contact. Five miles along the track, Cready-Smythe had pulled up. "What do you think? Do we chance the Oksu Valley road?" He looked at Brodie. "There might be military traffic on it even at this time of night."

"No alternative," Brodie replied. They peered at maps under the jeep lights. Just before the village of Shindy, a caravan trail ran east along the deep valley heading up to the Nezatash Pass. Their Belkuz rendezvous lay in a small valley branching off the main track, but over rough country. "We'll never get the vehicles up there," Cready-Smythe objected.

"We have to ditch them anyway before daylight," Brodie said. "We get as far as we can with them."

"What about trying the tunnel?" Shane asked.

"It's fifteen miles and we'd never make it over the mountains carrying Wang," Brodie said.

"Sheng says we can leave them," Cready-Smythe said.

"No—we go out together," Brodie said.

"Or not at all," Cready-Smythe grunted.

Before regaining their vehicle, Brodie and Shane looked back down the long valley where they could discern the flickering lights of the blaze; several detonations echoed along the valley, like small-arms fire, then a louder bang followed by two more. "Must be the armoury," Brodie commented.

"Did you see those terns?" she asked. "I cried when I heard them and saw them burn."

"I know," he said. "But it was the only thing to do if we wanted to destroy those viruses." He helped her into the cabin.

On the Oksu Valley road which ran south before forking to cross the Afghan frontier at two points, they became wedged between two half-tracked armoured vehicles in a long military convoy; it meant crawling at ten miles an hour, but it got them through a check-point without incident. However, as soon as they turned left off the metalled road, they hit trouble. Burov slithered off the track with the jeep when he tried to avoid a pile of scree. With no hope of recovering the vehicle, Brodie put it in gear, turned the key and pressed the accelerator on the floorboards with his hands to send the jeep catapulting into the torrent below. Three miles further on, he had to repeat the act with the truck, for a plank bridge had tumbled into the ravine it crossed and they had no hope of repairing it. Brodie, Cready-Smythe and Shane spent half an hour sifting through the records in the back, taking those dealing with the camp experiments and setting fire to the rest before pushing the truck over the edge. At the bottom, its diesel tank exploded and it burned.

Now, they had to slog painfully upwards over steep rock faced with loose slag and scree; they took turns to carry Wang on their backs. Shigo scouted the trail for them. They decided to bind the ankles of their three hostages with rope, giving them enough to take short strides but preventing them from making a run for it in the dark. Their prisoners also took the first turn at carrying the wounded Chinese, Dettwiler handing him over to Burov who passed him to the colonel. Brodie mapped their route while Cready-Smythe and Shane brought up the rear.

Belkuz, where they might find shelter and the Chinese contacts, lay seven miles up the valley. Too far to reach that night. It was three hours till dawn and at their climbing rate that meant three to four miles. At nine thousand feet in air that lacked the bite of oxygen and numbing cold, they had to halt every half-hour for ten minutes to recover their strength. A wind had sprung up and they climbed, bending into it and peering into the dust it sent spiralling round them. Just after four, when they were resting, Brodie and Cready-Smythe decided they could not risk marching during daylight and must look for a hiding-place, one they could defend if they had to. But in this valley, closed at its upper end, they searched for an hour before Shigo discovered a narrow cave on the south side of the deep valley. It had no water, though it would protect them from the fiercest heat during the day.

Once inside, they tied the three prisoners' hands in front of them. Shane had a look at Wang's wounded leg and side. Blood was leaking from the stitches in his chest wound, but he had no fever. She made him comfortable and fed him the sweet tea Shigo brewed on his stove. When they checked their rations, they had just enough for two meals—a little flour, butter, two tins of ham, two of corned beef and some tea. But they needed water, so before the sun rose Brodie took Shigo and went down the valley to bring back stream water.

When they reached the stream, they spotted further down the valley, a hamlet they had missed in the dark. Brodie waited while Shigo went to beg some bread and milk from the Tajik family. Just under an hour later he returned with a worried frown over his handsome face. "Is two choppers coming along Oksu Valley," he said, pointing to the area. "And soldiers about two miles down." Soon, Brodie heard the metallic racket of the helicopters as they approached; although he could not see them, he could imagine them hovering and darting behind the point where the valley doglegged and Shigo had gone to reconnoitre. "How long before they reach our cave?" he asked.

Shigo held up two fingers, then three. Yes, he would have said three hours himself. He cursed Wang's wound. But for that, they might have reached Belkuz before daybreak . . . they might have, even in daylight despite the patrolling aircraft and lookout posts. Drawing Shigo after him, they scrambled upwards. "Now listen, Shigo," he panted. "Say nothing to Shane or Smythe-sahib, but I will give you the papers. Remember the tunnel, Tashkurgan-way?" Shigo nodded. "You take them through there to Tashkurgan. Dr Huang and Wali will have passed that way. Ask for them and tell them about us. Understood?"

"Understood, Paul-sahib." Shigo looked at him. "I take Shane with me."

"She would never go."

Back in the cave, they said nothing about the soldiers or the helicopters. Brodie lured Cready-Smythe on to the hillside to allow Shigo to pick up the lab records and disappear. Only after he had gone, did he say quietly to the SIS man, "There's a new company of KGB border guards coming up the valley." He explained what Shigo had seen and the instructions he had given the Hunza. "We have to hold them off to give time for him to make ground or get over the frontier," he said.

"How much ammo do we have?" Cready-Smythe drawled.

"Two hundred rounds—half for the two revolvers and the other half for the machine-pistol."

"In that case, we only need three of those rounds."

"For Burov, Dettwiler and the colonel?"

Cready-Smythe nodded. "Sit them, one by one, at the cave entrance and threaten to blow their brains out if the KGB come within rifle range."

"There's still a snag," Brodie remarked. "Food and water." Cready-Smythe shrugged.

"We'll have to ration everything, and suffer."

XXII

THEY DECIDED TO say nothing to the Chinese or the Russians, but they could see Krotkov had guessed their plight; he seemed unworried by his own situation as though realizing they would get no further. Dettwiler apparently shared his optimism, for he had not said one word since his capture. However, Burov had been shaken by what had happened in the camp and obviously thought he might land on the other side of the frontier; he had a penitent air, as though he wished to justify his role as head of research at the bird farm, or expunge some of his personal guilt feelings. In reply to questions by Shane, he murmured that he had merely been doing pure research and unfortunately several birds had managed to break out of the sanctuary with the consequences that they knew. "You realize, of course, that never would we have adapted those techniques you saw to any evil purpose," he declared.

"That thought never even entered our heads," Cready-Smythe said with mordant sarcasm. "Who could have suspected for one minute that you were purposely contaminating birds in order to release them and spread lethal disease?"

"But those were not lethal viruses," Burov protested.

"No, but once having established the lab techniques you could have given birds anything from bubonic plague to flu—anything providing you had already vaccinated your own population against it."

"But these techniques are known . . ." Burov started to say when Dettwiler opened his mouth for the first time.

"Nikolai, tell them nothing," he shouted in Russian. "They're pumping you for information."

"Obviously Dr Dettwiler thinks these are state secrets," Cready-Smythe declared.

"They are state secrets," Colonel Krotkov put in, giving Burov a steely look.

"Were," Cready-Smythe corrected. "I think we can guess what you were up to, can't we, Paul and Dr Kingslake?"

Brodie nodded, then said, "But it was pretty clever what Burov and Dettwiler were doing, all the same. We thought they were probably using gene-splicing techniques to combine various viruses with harmless microbes that live normally in the gut of man and most animals and birds."

"Yes, but a couple of things baffled us," Shane put in. "How they were going to afford the time and money to infect individual birds with the virus, and how they could breed colonies of birds that would migrate at the right time to specific areas of the world."

"That's what our tame ornithologist and biologists failed to figure out as well," Cready-Smythe said.

"Well, they hit on a way of solving both problems with one technique," Shane said. "They were cloning the birds."

"Making them all identical, you mean?"

Shane nodded. "When we saw those three terns Paul trapped and realized they were absolutely identical, we began to realize what they were doing. They gave the virus to just one bird, then created a whole assembly-line of birds exactly like it."

"How?" Cready-Smythe queried.

"It's a complicated technique," Shane replied. "But what they did was strip out the genetic material from fertilized eggs and replace it with genetic material taken from the one bird infected with the virus. Then they merely hatched the cloned eggs."

"So all the birds were carrying the same virus."

Shane nodded. "They also used a male bird so that they had birds they could castrate to prevent them from breeding and sowing the virus in an uncontrolled way."

"And they didn't want female birds laying eggs that could be eaten as well as propagating infected birds," Brodie put in.

Shane was going to say something when they heard a clattering sound echo up and down their valley. "What's that?" she asked, and Cready-Smythe shook his head and shrugged his shoulders feigning ignorance yet knowing it meant the Russians were probably using the two helicopters to airlift the KGB company as near as possible to where they had lost the trail. But it might take them some time to spot their cave. To take her mind off the sound, he asked, "Was that why the birds all behaved the same way?"

Brodie seized on his question. "Exactly. And it meant Burov and Dettwiler could choose a bird with a known migration track—say from Siberia into India and Africa—and every member of its clone would instinctively follow the same flight plan."

"Ingenious, professor," Cready-Smythe conceded looking at Burov, who rewarded him with a sick smile. "You really thought of everything."

"We took every precaution," Burov said.

"I bet you did," Cready-Smythe agreed. "Or you might have got into trouble if your birds had come home to roost around the Kremlin and you had given the whole of the Politburo Pink-eye or shingles." Cready-Smythe helped himself to one of his special Bond Street cigarettes, now the worse for wear having lain in the bottom of his knapsack. "I suppose that's why you got them to migrate in midsummer."

"No, that wasn't the only reason," Brodie put in. "They were doing dummy runs and wanted to keep track of their birds which they couldn't have done in the migration season."

"They still had to pull the migration trick."

"Did you see those terns?" Brodie asked. "They had fooled them into believing it was autumn!"

"Fooled them! How?"

"Well, birds usually migrate to their winter quarters after the breeding season, in the autumn. And one of the things that triggers the migration impulse is the length of the days."

"Ah! those domed bird-houses," Cready-Smythe exclaimed. "They played about with artificial light and shortened or lengthened the days in order to dupe the birds."

"That was only one thing," Brodie conceded. "But those birdhouses were also air-conditioned so that they could raise or lower the temperature to simulate summer or winter climate for various birds, another factor that influences migration."

"They were doing hormone work, too," Shane put in.

"That was their third trick," Brodie said. "They fed the birds small dozes of thyroid and pituitary hormone, two substances that migrating birds produce naturally, and this also helped to fatten them for their long flight." He turned to Burov. "Am I right, professor?" he asked. Burov said nothing, though his expression confirmed Brodie's statements.

"Seems they have thought of everything," Cready-Smythe remarked. "If they were going to use those birds in a war situation, they had to be able to control their migration flights and send them out in any season." A grin penetrated his battered face as he looked at Dettwiler, then at Burov. "What species were you going to use as your real biological missiles, professor? The American eagle, the bird of paradise, the shrike, the English robin, or the homespun sparrow?"

Burov did not reply.

XXIII

JUST AFTER TWO o'clock, they spotted the first soldiers climbing the steep sides of the valley on either side of the stream bed; they were taking no chances, covering each other and leapfrogging towards the hillside where the eight people were hiding; in the broiling heat, they moved laboriously. However, it seemed likely that within another hour they would reach and surround the cave. Cready-Smythe took the Chinese machine-pistol, armed and set it for single-shots; he took aim at one of the steel helmets between two rocks five hundred feet below them and placed three bullets within five yards of the man who took cover. At once, a volley of shots sprayed the rocks around them, one of them burying itself in the back of the cave. "Dangerous," Brodie murmured.

"You had better tell them not to be so stupid, colonel," Cready-Smythe drawled, pushing Krotkov forward to the cave mouth in full view of the soldiers. "They might kill you." Krotkov's parade-ground bellow rang down the valley, ordering the troops to stop firing.

"Better explain to them if they try to attack, we shall begin by shooting you, then Dr Dettwiler and finally Professor Burov," Cready-Smythe prompted. Krotkov relayed this message. Someone with a loud-hailer answered. "Sounds like our friend, Tikonov," Brodie said. "He's telling them to offer us safe passage in exchange for the three prisoners."

"Of course, he means safe passage to a cell in Lubyanka Jail, the KGB headquarters in Moscow," Cready-Smythe drawled. "Order him to pay us a courtesy call, colonel—we promise not to shoot him."

Colonel Krotkov roared the instruction and a few minutes later, a white handkerchief fluttered over a pile of glacier moraine and a hesitant figure began to climb, hand over foot, towards them.

Twenty yards from the cave, Cready-Smythe called on him to halt; he pushed Krotkov, Dettwiler and Burov before him to the cave entrance, menacing them with a revolver. "We just wanted you to see for yourself we mean what we say," he shouted to the Russian major. "Any attempt to take us prisoner and we shall shoot all three of these men. Understood?"

"Understood," Tikonov called back. As he turned to retreat downhill, Dettwiler suddenly bawled something at him, and Tikonov raised a hand in acknowledgement.

"What did he say?" Cready-Smythe asked Brodie.

"That we've water and food for two days at the most."

Cready-Smythe brought his fist down on the back of Dettwiler's neck, dropping him senseless. "He can take the first stint at the cave entrance," he said, handing the revolver to Sheng instructing the Chinese to sit behind the Russian and shoot him if he made a move. Sheng only wanted the excuse.

From mid-morning, it turned hot but in the afternoon the heat had become unbearable, reaching into the deepest part of the cave and making breathing difficult; it reminded them they were living at eleven thousand feet in the world's highest and driest cordillera. If they did not sweat openly, they were losing water and had only two pints each for their needs—to cut their thirst, cook and brew tea. Shane and Brodie rationed the food and cooked flour pancakes to go with their corned-beef. "I wonder if Shigo has made it," Shane whispered. Brodie was asking himself the same question; he hoped Shigo would not take too many chances if he travelled by day; it seemed from the sound of a helicopter behind their hill and several MIG fighters overhead that the Russians were stepping up their patrols.

They were glad when the sun sank below the line of the vast Fedchenko Glacier and the Lenin Peak and darkness brought a cool breeze into the cave. Shane relieved the Chinaman with orders to fire one shot every hour to let the Russians know they were keeping vigil. For greater security, Brodie and Cready-Smythe took turns to sit on the hillside above the cave with the machine-pistol armed to ensure no-one would surprise them from that quarter. Before sunset they had been sweating; but within an hour, they were shivering, huddling together in the cave for warmth and even daring to light their gas stove and expend their precious fuel to keep warm. With what remained of the corned-beef, they made soup, thickening it with flour; this helped to combat the cold and tedium. Cready-Smythe divided his whisky and, much to Sheng's disgust, offered the Russians an equal share. He, Shane and Brodie gave some of their ration to Wang whose chest wound now showed signs of infection and they wondered if he were losing blood internally. "He's got three degrees of temperature," Shane whispered. "Another night or two here and I wouldn't say much for his chances of pulling through."

"We can arrange for the Russians to evacuate him if he gets worse."

"No," Sheng snapped. "Wang stays here. If he dies, I kill one of those in his memory." He pointed the revolver, from which he refused to be separated, at the colonel and the two scientists.

When dawn filtered into the valley, they saw Tikonov and his platoons had not budged from their positions; on the morning breeze, they even caught the smell of frying eggs coming up the valley. They themselves ate tinned ham and pancakes. Their quartermaster, Cready-Smythe, said they had water for a day and a half and food for twenty-four hours. "Then what?" Brodie asked.

"We bargain our way out."

"They won't wear that."

"All right, then we cross our fingers that Her Majesty's government has two or three spies they can trade off for us."

That day turned into a long purgatory as the sun swung slowly through the sultry, grey sky. Through his loud-hailer, Tikonov urged them every hour to surrender, promising them fair treatment. They replied with several shots. Although not daring to venture out of their cave, they sensed the area was surrounded by troops. "You will have to lay down your arms sooner or later," Colonel Krotkov said as he took his place at the cave mouth.

Brodie agreed with him, if only because Wang's condition was growing worse by the hour; either he talked deliriously or lapsed into long silences while Shane fed him sips of water laced with whisky. Lack of water and food, as well as the enervating heat, was telling on everybody. Even Cready-Smythe sounded despondent as he beckoned Brodie aside and whispered, "Do you think Shigo has managed to make it across the frontier?"

Brodie had witnessed the Hunza cover fifteen to twenty miles a day in the worst mountains of the Karakorams and Hindu Kush ranges, much more rugged country than the Pamirs. "He'll get there if anybody can," he replied, then looked quizzically at his old boss. "You're not thinking of chucking your hand in, are you?"

Before Cready-Smythe could reply, they heard the clicking, sing-song voice of Wang; he was babbling deliriously, then moaning. Sheng got up from his corner and crossed to take his compatriot's hand and whisper something in his ear. Whatever he said did not stop the raving which seemed all the more poignant in that high-pitched tone.

Cready-Smythe thumbed at the wounded man. "I'm just thinking that if he dies and Sheng cuts loose with that revolver, our friend Tikonov will do us all in and we'll have done all this for nothing."

"So, we surrender," Brodie said.

However, they did not need to put their decision into effect. After nightfall, as they were cooking their scant rations and Cready-Smythe was preparing to mount guard, three objects flew in an arc into the cave; one knocked over a mess tin on the small stove, a second hit Krotkov and the third landed at the back of the cave; in a second, three flashes lit the dark hole, blinding everyone there; then it seemed the whole cave erupted and collapsed on them as three cataclysmic bangs followed the flashes. For fully a minute afterwards everyone seemed paralysed by the lightning flashes and the thunder that followed them. No-one moved as the cave filled with Tikonov and half a dozen of his men, all armed with Kalashnikov machine-pistols.

First, Tikonov helped his colonel up and untied his bonds; his men bound the five prisoners' hands behind their backs and cut the two scientists free. As soon as Dettwiler had his hands freed, he strode over to where Cready-Smythe stood with Brodie and, in front of everyone, drew out and smashed a fist into the SIS man's face. Cready-Smythe went down in a heap at Brodie's feet, moaning with pain. "That's for the one you gave me," Dettwiler snapped.

"How many of our men are dead in the camp, Tikonov?" Krotkov asked.

"Eight, colonel—but thirteen are badly burned and they've been flown to a hospital in Murgab."

"And our camp?"

Tikonov turned and fixed Brodie with a look of absolute hatred. "I should kill him now," he said through clenched teeth. He shook his head at Krotkov. "There is almost nothing left," he muttered.

"My birds?" Burov queried.

"Dead—every one of them."

One soldier arrived with a pressure lamp, another with a small stove. Tikonov pointed to Wang who had not stirred and did not seem to realize they had been captured. "With the Chinaman it is too difficult to make the descent in the dark, colonel. We can heat and light this place and stay here until dawn." Krotkov nodded agreement.

More troops arrived with another stove and blankets which they issued to everyone. They brought up hot soup and stew. "It's better than we'll get in Moscow," Cready-Smythe murmured as he mopped up his stew, two-handed, with a piece of rye bread.

An hour after dawn, when they had eaten breakfast, Tikonov had their hands freed but kept rope shackles on their legs. "You will carry the Chinaman between you," he ordered, pointing to a makeshift stretcher and a coil of rope to tie Wang to it. When Brodie and Cready-Smythe had secured the wounded man, two of Tikonov's men prodded them with their bayonet points, motioning them to pick up the stretcher and start downhill.

Without the dead weight of the Chinaman and their own rucksacks, that march would have exhausted them; with them, it became a calvary. Over some of the rougher rock outcrops, they had to make a rope sling and lower the stretcher to Sheng and Shane, for the Russians refused to help but waited and watched on Tikonov's orders. On two occasions when they laid their burden down to rest, Tikonov himself forced them to pick it up and continue, cuffing them across the face until they complied. As the steep, enclosed valley filled with the furnace heat of the sun, Tikonov and his men began to tire. At midday, they stopped by a small hamlet of two mud-brick houses with thatched shelters for the animals; two Tajik farmers supplied them with unleavened bread, their wives roasted half a goat and distributed this with vegetables, then peaches and apricots from their orchards to boost the army rations; someone went and fetched milk from the Kirghiz yurts a mile across the valley where a large herd of sheep and goats browsed.

As they ate, Colonel Krotkov and Tikonov talked in Russian, unaware that Brodie understood them. From what they said, it seemed they had orders to take the prisoners back to the burnt-out camp where they would be interrogated by KGB chiefs before being transferred by helicopter to a military airfield and flown to Moscow. Tikonov explained they had left their three trucks some seven to eight miles down the valley. Brodie relayed all this in whispers to Cready-Smythe. Both agreed that, once back in the camp they would have no chance of escaping. They must try to seize one of the three trucks and make a dash for the Afghan border.

When they had eaten and rested, the march resumed. Though the terrain had improved, they still crawled along, impeded by the brazen heat and the altitude. Shane and the other Chinaman each took a handle of the stretcher to give the other two men some respite. All this time, Wang never once opened his eyes; his face looked like old vellum and only when he moaned did they realize he was still alive. At five o'clock, they sighted the three trucks, guarded by five men of Tikonov's company about a mile west of the place where the jeep had fallen into the ravine. Three tents sat beside the vehicles on level terrain beside the stream and caravan trail. On their approach the detachment began to strike camp and load their tents and equipment into the trucks, evidently preparing to leave immediately the main party arrived.

When they reached the trucks, Tikonov ordered his men to bind the hands of the four prisoners. As they did this, the clatter of a helicopter reached them, the sound coming from a machine flying south along the Oksu Valley, following the route they had taken from the camp. As they spotted it, the helicopter turned left and headed into their valley; but before it arrived, two MIG fighters appeared to escort the machine; they streaked over the camp a few hundred feet up, dipping their wings in some sort of signal. Tikonov gazed at Colonel Krotkov who shook his head in puzzlement. "There must have been some change in plan," he muttered.

Within minutes the MI 9 helicopter, with its Red Army star and markings, was hovering over the field, its great fan blowing dust in their faces. Immediately it darted down, the door slid back and out stepped two men; one wore the uniform of an air-force staff colonel and had the build and flat features of some Turki natives of this part of Russia; his companion had the swarthy, gypsy face of a Georgian or an Armenian. Both glanced upwards at the two MIGs which were circling a few thousand feet above them before walking over to the colonel and Tikonov and saluting them. "Our respects, Comrade Colonel Krotkov, and our congratulations for the capture of these five spies who have destroyed your camp," the staff colonel said. While speaking, he produced a document from his leather briefcase, opened it then paused, conscious of the eyes fixed on the bit of paper. He went on: "First, allow me to present Comrade Aram Petrosian, delegate from the Committee on State Security, who has just arrived from Moscow. I am Colonel Georgi Arsenevich Orazberdieff of the Murgab military district." He handed his document to Krotkov. "This order, signed by General Vladimir Ivanovich Orloff, commanding the district, is our authority to escort the five spies and saboteurs to Murgab. There,

Comrade Commissar Petrosian will conduct them by military aircraft to Moscow where your superiors are waiting to interrogate them."

Krotkov accepted the order and read it slowly and carefully. Watching from three yards away, Brodie could see his face cloud with doubt. "So, this comes from General Orloff," he mused. His eyes flicked towards the helicopter, sitting with its single screw rotating slowly, then he looked upwards at the two MIGs wheeling overhead. Tikonov and a dozen of his men were standing, waiting for orders.

"Good," Krotkov said, finally, handing back the paper. "You may take charge of the spies, Comrade Colonel."

As the civilian commissar and the staff colonel turned to give instructions, Krotkov murmured something out of the side of his mouth to Tikonov, who dropped his hand towards his revolver. At that moment, Brodie yelled a warning to the two men; with his hands still tied, he could only put his head down and make a lunge at Tikonov before he could reach his gun or bellow an order to his men; Brodie sank his head as far as it would go into Tikonov's paunch, knocked him off balance and they both went over in a tangle of arms and legs. On hearing the shout, both the colonel and the commissar threw themselves flat. As Tikonov was falling, he grabbed Brodie round the waist with one hand while the other clamped round the revolver at his side. Brodie realized the KGB major meant to use him as a shield and shoot the two men on the ground; he thrust upwards with his bound hands, breaking Tikonov's hold on him, then twisted his body to the left and pushed with both feet to free himself.

Before Tikonov could get a shot off, the crack of a rifle came from the helicopter. Brodie heard the thump of the heavy slug smashing into Tikonov's chest; its impact seemed to pick him several inches off the ground then bang him back again; a second bullet smashed through his jaw. A cry of agony choked in his throat and his big mujik hand went to his neck from which blood was spurting. It got only to his shoulder before it fell back, twitched and lay still. Tikonov was dead. No-one had time to react before two bursts of machine-pistol fire racketed over the heads of Colonel Krotkov and the KGB platoon.

"On your bellies," a Russian voice commanded from the helicopter, and the men dropped and stayed still. "The first man to move will be shot and the colonel with him," the voice bawled. As if to ram home this warning, the two watching MIGs suddenly swooped and flew wingtip to wingtip, a few hundred feet above the camp as though they had been alerted by radio.

Both the commissar and the staff colonel had risen to their feet and now had revolvers in their hands. "Get in, quickly," Colonel Orazberdieff ordered, pointing Sheng and the others towards the helicopter. "You, too, Comrade Colonel," he said, waving his revolver at Krotkov.

Within a minute they had hoisted Wang into the machine, pushed Krotkov after him then entered themselves followed by the colonel and commissar. At the door, Colonel Orazberdieff turned and shouted, "Any attempt to fire on us and I shall shoot your colonel and order the two fighters to attack you."

Not a man budged as they lifted off and their rotors raised dust all round the troops lying flat on the ground. Looking out of a porthole, the last thing Brodie saw was the twisted corpse of Major Tikonov, a broken marionette. With the rotor shadow flickering over it, it seemed the body still trembled with life.

Everything had happened so quickly that none of them could believe they had been rescued and were sitting in a Russian-built helicopter being escorted out of the Soviet Union by two Russian-built MIG jet fighters. Yet, within twenty minutes, they had flown down the Oksu Valley and were crossing into Afghanistan through one of the northern passes; they followed the river valley through Afghanistan until they picked out the tributary that ran nearly to the Irshad Pass and the Pakistan frontier. Nothing challenged them as they trundled along the pass and across the frontier. Once safely over, the two MIGs dipped their wings in salute and left them to head back into Sinkiang and their home base in China.

From the colonel and the commissar (both Turki members of the

Chinese state security police in Sinkiang) they learned that Dr Huang and Wali had crossed the frontier two days before. By flying their disguised MIGs across the frontier and using high-altitude reconnaissance aircraft, they had managed to monitor roughly what was happening in the camp; they had observed the avalanches, the explosions and fire. Twelve hours ago, Shigo had appeared through the tunnel to inform them where they were hiding and how they risked capture. So, the Chinese had altered their original plan to pick them up at Belkuz, they had watched them trek down the valley and waited their opportunity to airlift them out.

"And you knew back there this wasn't a Russian helicopter and those were Chinese fighter planes," Shane protested.

"We had a rough idea," Cready-Smythe answered, then grinned at her. "But you can thank Paul. He fixed that ploy with the Chinese that night they came into Hunza." He pointed to the staff colonel and the commissar. "But I admit those two almost had me fooled."

"You might have let me into your little secret," Shane exclaimed with some bitterness.

"What if they had tortured you in the camp?" Cready-Smythe came back.

Brodie cut short their argument by thumbing through the porthole at Runghar, the village where the story had begun with the outbreak of shingles. They landed on the very island where they had pitched their tent on that first trip. There, the staff colonel saluted them, explaining he had to get his wounded superior, Wang, to hospital at Kashgar then have Colonel Krotkov conducted across the Sino-Soviet border to Murgab.

However, someone was waiting for them on the island: Shigo. They had flown him over the Mintaka Pass that morning and dropped him here. He had acquired four ponies for their trip through the gorges to the Hunza Valley the next day. He told them the Chinese had wanted the papers he carried, but he said they belonged to Smythe-sahib and would only let them copy the documents. "You're a wonder, Shigo," Cready-Smythe exclaimed, grabbing the pile of paper. "You know, I think I'll recruit you and take you back to London with me."

"No you won't," Shane snapped before she realized all three were grinning at her and the idea.

XXIV

IT TOOK TIME to put their nightmare behind them. All four had taut, drawn faces that contrasted sharply with the relaxed smiles and unhurried rhythm of the Hunza people. On their first meeting, Brodie could see the old wazir scrutinize them as though confirming the truth of the legend—that those who left the valley, even for as little as two weeks, felt their years exact their true toll. However, they were back. And Hunza did seem a hermetic world where the valley, the mountains towering over it and the sky above them had an immemorial stamp, and time did seem to run slower than elsewhere. Shane's face softened, her dark hair and smile regained their lustre; even Cready-Smythe appeared in no hurry to take the trail to Gilgit and fly back to 'Pindi and to London. "I wonder if they drug these apricots, Paul," he said with his ingenuous grin.

He spent days leafing through the papers they had stolen from the camp, badgering them with questions about ornithology and molecular biology, encoding and decoding yards of messages and using Shigo as his courier between Baltit and Gilgit. He flew to Gilgit himself to catch a plane for Kashgar in Sinkiang and confer with some high-ranking Chinese security man. But two weeks after their return, he announced his departure. "If I stay any longer, the place will get me, too," he said.

"Heaven forbid," Shane exclaimed.

They were sitting, dining on the terrace the evening before his departure. A red sun and a blue sky had fused their colours to create mauve and purple tints in the great glaciers sheeting the face of Rakaposhi, and the clouds round its top. None of them had felt like talking about their expedition, but now Shane brought it up. "Do you really believe the Russians would have used those birds in biological warfare?" she asked.

"They build arsenals of nuclear bombs and lethal chemicals."

"But beautiful and innocent creatures like birds," she persisted.

"Why not?" Cready-Smythe said. "Before any shooting war, there's a period of sabre-rattling, and if we hadn't rumbled them, the Russians might have used that phase to spread really serious diseases among potential enemies—diseases like plague, cholera, smallpox, flu. And who would have guessed where the diseases came from?"

"And do you think we've stopped them?"

Cready-Smythe nodded, though he did not elaborate. It was Brodie who answered the question. "He'll circulate the information among every United Nations delegation, backing it up with the papers we brought out and with Chinese corroboration."

"Watch it, Paul."

Brodie ignored him. "From now on, every country in the world will have its official bird-watchers looking out for the sort of genetic tricks Burov and Dettwiler were playing." He looked at Cready-Smythe. "He can do something else—threaten that the Pakistanis, who don't much like the Russians, will put the bogus Dr Bolanz and his five men on trial and create an international sensation that will blacken the Soviet name for all time. Think of bird-lovers . . ."

"Paul has a vivid imagination," Cready-Smythe murmured.

"Thank God," Shane said. She rose and went indoors to fetch their coffee. When she returned, she said, "Perhaps I shouldn't mention this, but I almost felt sorry for Krotkov."

"They'll find him a billet in Outer Mongolia, I expect."

"And Burov—what'll happen to him?"

"He'll get his knuckles rapped for talking too much, but he's too important to send into Siberia."

"I should think Dettwiler will probably get his job," Shane commented, then saw the smile on Brodie's face. "Have I said something daft?" she asked.

"No," he said, turning again to Cready-Smythe. "I'd say Shane hit it right on the nail, wouldn't you?"

"What are you two driving at?" Shane cried, exasperated.

"Tell her," Brodie urged. "Tell her you weren't worried about what happened to Burov or Krotkov, and why."

Cready-Smythe's coffee cup rattled in its saucer and he spluttered through the mouthful he took as though the liquid had burned him. "I was only worried about us," he protested.

"And Dettwiler, or whatever his Russian name is."

"Dettwiler!" Shane exclaimed, observing that the name had effaced the humour from Cready-Smythe's face. "But he was the biggest villain of the lot," she went on. "You even knocked him out."

"The first time I'd ever seen him use physical violence," Brodie said. "If I hadn't already picked up one or two hints I might have been fooled by that little performance."

"Performance! You mean, Dettwiler was working for him?" Shane pointed at Cready-Smythe, who now looked wooden-faced. When Brodie nodded, she stared, incredulously. "He had a man in that camp all the time and didn't let on!"

"He couldn't do that without the risk of giving Dettwiler away, could he now?" Brodie replied, looking hard at Cready-Smythe.

"An interesting supposition, Paul," the SIS man came back, smoothly, recovering his poise. "But you've got nothing to back it."

"Dettwiler was the only man who knew we were at Runghar, and I would imagine he passed that information on to you," Brodie said. "I'd say he used your friend, Ahmed, as his Afghan contact."

"And behold, Mr Cready-Smythe suddenly materializes in Delhi," Shane said, sarcastically.

"We had the World Health Organization evidence, some of it from yourselves," Cready-Smythe countered.

"But nothing to indicate where the birds came from," Brodie put in. "You got that from Ahmed through Dettwiler and only then did you begin looking for birds and setting up your satellite scans—that's how it happened."

"A nice theory."

"More than that," Brodie came back. "Dettwiler even passed you the Russian code-name for the operation—PROJECT ICARUS—and you put it in that file you keep in your room."

"You're talking nonsense," Cready-Smythe snapped, now nettled. "And it's dangerous nonsense at that. If the Chinese or anybody else got hold of that story . . ."

"The Chinese would be more annoyed if they guessed you led them on that patrol with the intention of more or less walking into the camp."

"He gave himself up!" Shane gasped.

"I told you, Paul's got too much imagination," Cready-Smythe said, blandly. "Those two wogs were blundering about in the dark like elephants. How was I to know they both had night blindness, or lack of vitamin A, or something?"

"Why did you do it?" Shane asked. Neither Cready-Smythe nor Brodie said anything, and she went on, "I know why. You realized Paul would come in after you or find a way of rescuing you and your precious papers. You left everything to Paul."

"I would only have got in his way."

"Why didn't you get one of your own boys to go with you?"

Cready-Smythe looked at her straight and hard. "I wouldn't trust anybody else with my life," he said.

"And Paul's life?"

"Let's say we trust each other, and if we went in there with different motives, we had the same aim—to save lives."

"But you were only interested in some lives, Paul in life itself."

Cready-Smythe left her the last word. Anyway, there seemed no more to say. All three sat there until darkness had crept up out of the valley and lapped their feet and he excused himself to go and finish his packing. He was leaving with Shigo two hours before dawn, having made the surprising decision to trek to Gilgit. Shane put out a hand to grasp Brodie's as though for reassurance. She murmured, "Do you think we've seen the last of that man?" Brodie gazed after the long silhouette disappearing into the old palace, and shrugged his shoulders non-committally. But something whispered that Cready-Smythe would turn up again and, even if he dared not admit it to Shane, he would be sorry if it were otherwise.